HOME NO MORE

Emma thought she would be a wealthy heiress when her father died. Instead she is shocked to find she faces the prospect of having to sell the home she loves. John Burroughs is willing to help the lonely girl with this painful task, but what about Jed Riley, the wheeler and dealer from Liverpool with an eye for antiques? Which man really cares about Emma and which one has other motives?

SHEILA HOLROYD

HOME NO MORE

Complete and Unabridged

LINFORD
Leicester

First published in Great Britain in 2006

First Linford Edition
published 2007

British Library CIP Data

Holroyd, Sheila
   Home no more.—Large print ed.—
   Linford romance library
   1. Love stories
   2. Large type books
   I. Title
   823.9'14 [F]

   ISBN 978–1–84617–758–3

Published by
F. A. Thorpe (Publishing)
Anstey, Leicestershire

Set by Words & Graphics Ltd.
Anstey, Leicestershire
Printed and bound in Great Britain by
T. J. International Ltd., Padstow, Cornwall

This book is printed on acid-free paper

1

Mrs Wrenshaw shivered, pulled her fur jacket round her more closely, and cast a quick glance round the church.

'Not many people here,' she commented, making it sound like Emma's fault.

'It's not surprising,' her niece defended herself. 'Father was ill for some time, remember. He lost contact with most of his friends.'

Not that he ever had many, she reminded herself. Roger Digby had been sharp-tongued and bad-tempered, characteristics which had alienated most people, including his wife, who had abandoned husband and baby daughter in favour of a racing driver and then vanished without trace after the driver had abandoned her.

'Still, the Digbys have been at Park Hall for a hundred-and-fifty years and the family have always been leading figures in the town,' Mrs Wrenshaw complained. 'You would have thought that the mayor or the deputy mayor would have thought it their duty to attend my brother's funeral.'

Obviously these dignitaries had decided they had better things to do than spend the morning in the parish church, and when the organist started to play and the service began, there was only a handful of mourners present to say farewell to Roger Digby, and even fewer stood by the graveside in the fitful Cheshire sunshine while his coffin was lowered into the grave.

Emma had arranged for refreshments to be available at the local Conservative club after the funeral.

Mrs Wrenshaw, who had had little contact with her brother for several years, was eager to get back to her comfortable home in Surrey and soon drew Emma aside.

'I would stay if I thought you needed me,' she told her, 'but you are obviously a very competent young woman, and I would only be in the way.' She hesitated. 'Of course, now you'll have to decide what you are going to do in the future. I suppose you could go back to college. If you ever need somewhere to stay, however — for a short time — please feel free to contact us.'

Emma dutifully thanked her. 'But I know how busy you are, Aunt Joan, so I don't want to impose on you.'

She tried not to laugh as she saw her aunt's expression of relief, kissed her on the cheek, and saw her to the taxi that would take her to the station. The club was almost empty when she returned, and she was just thinking thankfully that she would soon be free to leave when the door opened and the comfortable figure of George Stanford, her father's solicitor, walked in.

She smiled in greeting, and then stared in open curiosity at the young man who accompanied him. He was tall, fair-haired, with a firm chin and the tan of a sportsman. His elegant dark grey suit was eminently suitable for a funeral, but his tie was a vivid silk concoction in scarlet and yellow. As he saw her looking at him, his hand went up self-consciously to cover his neckwear.

George Stanford murmured the appropriate words of condolence and introduced the stranger as his nephew, John Burroughs, who shook Emma's hand and smiled at her apologetically.

'I'm sorry about the tie,' he told her. 'Uncle George didn't tell me I'd be coming here, or I would have worn something more suitable.'

He was the only person so far that day who had looked at her as if he saw her as a person in her own right and not just as Roger Digby's daughter, and she forgave him his sartorial indiscretion immediately.

George Stanford was looking round. 'I thought your aunt was staying to help you for a few days?'

'I'm afraid you've just missed her. There wasn't really anything for her to do and she was anxious to get home.'

The solicitor nodded. 'I see. So you are coming to see me on your own tomorrow?' He looked grave. 'There is a lot to discuss.'

The meeting to discuss her father's will was one more formality to be completed. She knew her father had left everything to her, so once Mr Stanford had told her how much that was, she could start to plan her future. The modern Digby family might no longer possess the immense fortune of the Victorian Digby who had bought Park Hall, but her grandfather had sold the family tool manufacturing company and divided the proceeds between his two children, so to the best of her knowledge she should have no financial worries.

So the news George Stanford gave her in his comfortably old-fashioned office was therefore completely unexpected.

'Nothing?' she said incredulously. 'No money at all?'

The solicitor shook his head sympathetically.

'None. Didn't your father ever discuss business affairs with you?'

She shook her head. 'He liked to be in control of matters like that. He did say occasionally that he would explain everything to me sometime, but he never got round to it.'

'But he was ill for some time. He must have realised that you would have to cope with all these matters eventually.'

'He didn't accept that he was going to die. He always thought that some treatment, some new discovery, would cure him. And the end came suddenly.'

Mr Stanford leaned back in his big chair and regarded her silently for some time before suddenly leaning forward briskly.

'I'd better tell you the worst now rather than spin it out. Not only has your father not left you any money, there are debts that must be paid.'

She looked at him, confused. 'But if

there is no money, how can I do that?'

He shrugged, as if to say that it was not his concern, then looked at her downcast face and apparently took pity on her.

'Emma, our firm has acted as your family's solicitors for many years and your father made us his executors, but for the last ten years we have had little to do with him, and it was only when I started to go through the papers I have obtained since he died that I realised what a mess his affairs were in.

'Now you buried your father only yesterday, so you are in no state to take in all the details. Go home, have a rest and a good night's sleep, and I'll call tomorrow to arrange another meeting.'

John Burroughs was chatting to the receptionist and his uncle hailed him gratefully.

'John, you've got your car outside. Will you give Miss Digby a lift home? It's less than five minutes.'

His nephew straightened up with

alacrity. 'I shall be delighted. This way, Miss Digby.'

His car was a small, sleek sports car, and it distracted Emma from the news she had just received. She regarded it with delight.

'It's beautiful!' she said sincerely. 'It must be fun to drive.'

He looked smug. 'It is. My uncle says it is an unjustified extravagance, but I love it. What do you drive?'

She grimaced and wrinkled her nose. 'An eighteen-year-old little car, designed for French farmers and very practical, but not exciting.'

'You'll have to give me instructions how to get to your house. Incidentally, who's there at the moment?'

'No-one.'

He turned his head towards her in horror. 'You mean you are going back to an empty house? I can't allow that! Let me take you somewhere, or we can just go for a ride. You can see how this car goes then.'

She was tempted. She had just been

given devastating news and some time she would have to go home and think about it, but surely she could enjoy a little distraction first?

'Well, people round here might think it odd if they saw me out driving just a day after my father's funeral, but we could go to Anscale Hall. It's an old house with beautiful gardens and they are open to the public. It's about ten miles from here.'

The car park at Anscale Hall was nearly full, a fact that was explained by bright yellow posters informing the world that the Manor was hosting an antiques fair that day. However, John Burroughs declared a lack of interest in antiques and instead they strolled through the gardens, now in their full early summer beauty.

She learned that John (they were on first name terms by now) had gone to a minor public school, then lived most of his life in London, but had recently moved to a flat in Manchester and worked in finance.

He began to look round. 'I don't know about you, but I'm beginning to feel hungry. Let's find the tea room.'

In five minutes she was working her way through a full afternoon tea. John watched her indulgently and even surrendered his own scone when he saw her eyeing it greedily.

'I was too busy to have breakfast,' she apologised.

Then John looked up, a curious expression crossed his face and Emma heard a voice behind her.

'John? John Burroughs? I thought you avoided the countryside.'

Turning, Emma saw a man aged about thirty, with shaggy black hair and dressed so casually in jeans and a sweatshirt that he bordered on scruffiness. He was deeply tanned, and showed brilliant white teeth as he grinned at John, who was smiling politely.

'Miss Digby, may I introduce Jed Riley. We were at school together.' He looked back at the newcomer. 'I suppose you are here for the antiques.'

'Of course.' Jed Riley's grin widened as he looked from John to Emma. 'And I take it you are here for pleasure?'

Emma noticed the strong Liverpool accent.

'Miss Digby's father was buried yesterday morning. I thought a drive might help her,' John said stiffly.

Emma was taken aback by the stranger's reaction to the news. There was real pain on his face. 'I'm sorry, Miss Digby. I know what it's like when you've just lost someone you love.'

His sympathy stirred her emotions. She felt a sudden pang of grief for her father, and realised that she had been so busy dealing with practical matters since his death that she had not given herself time to mourn.

With an effort she summoned a smile. 'There's no need to apologise, Mr Riley. How were you to know? Anyway, thank you for your sympathy.'

'I won't intrude any more,' and he was gone, slipping easily away through the crowded room, and Emma turned back to John, full of curiosity.

'Did you say he was at school with you? He doesn't look the public school type.'

John's lips tightened. 'He was there because of some scheme which gave students from state schools who showed exceptional promise the chance to come to a public school.'

'So Jed was very bright?'

'He was supposed to be,' John admitted a little grudgingly, 'but he dropped out before the Sixth Form. I suppose he didn't fit in.'

'What does he do?'

'He wheels and deals,' John said a little obscurely. 'I believe he buys and sells antiques among other things. We run across each other occasionally. He sold a picture for me once and got a good price for it, though he charged a hefty commission.'

He leaned forward. 'Forget about Jed Riley. I've told you a lot about me, now it is your turn.'

She told him her story, conscious of how dull it sounded. After her mother had left them, her father had sent her to boarding school at the earliest possible age. At eighteen she had left school and started to train as a teacher, but towards the end of the first year, she was summoned home because her father had fallen ill, and she nursed him for the following eighteen months until he died.

'I think that is why I'm not as distressed by his death and funeral as I expected to be. We were never close, and I knew for months that he was going to die, so there was no shock.'

'And you were on your own? Haven't you got any family?'

'Only my aunt, and she and my father were never on close terms.'

He frowned, shaking his head. 'You must have been very lonely.'

'Not that I was aware of. I've become very self-reliant over the years. When I wasn't looking after my father, I read and gardened.'

'You like gardens?'

She nodded emphatically. 'I love gardens, and Cheshire is full of beautiful gardens like Anscale Hall. The gardens at Park Hall were famous in Victorian times, and I used to dream of restoring them. There are plenty of old photographs showing what they used to be like.'

John caught the wistful note in her voice. 'What's stopping you? Park Hall is yours and you are free now to do what you like.'

She grimaced. 'Restoring gardens is expensive. Ask the National Trust.'

'You haven't got enough money to do it?'

'I haven't any money,' she said bleakly. 'That was what your uncle told me today.'

'I see,' he said slowly. 'That explains why my uncle was so nervous and short-tempered this morning. He's a nice man and he doesn't like breaking bad news.'

'I have big problems and I don't

know what to do. You work in finance, so can you give me any advice?'

He sat up, looking businesslike. 'All right, you haven't got cash. But you have got a large house that your family has lived in for a long time. How about pictures, furniture?'

She looked at him unbelievingly. 'Sell the furniture?'

He looked at her patiently. 'You say you need money. Selling a few pieces may give you the cash you want. The alternative . . . ' He hesitated.

'Go on!'

'The alternative is to sell Park Hall.'

Her first impulse was to put her hands over her ears to shut out his words. Park Hall was her home, the one secure comforting factor in her life. She could not lose it.

As they left the tea rooms, Emma heard a voice calling her and when she looked round she saw a figure waving at her.

'Lord Anscale!' she exclaimed warmly, and went to greet the owner of Anscale

Hall, a tall man dressed in well-worn tweeds. Her father had known him slightly and she had met him frequently at events such as garden shows. Now he held her hands comfortingly.

'I was sorry to hear about your father's death, Emma. If you feel in the need of a little company you can always come over here, you know.'

She thanked him, and introduced John, who seemed a little too impressed at being introduced to the rich landowner, and Emma felt that he had not made a good impression on Lord Anscale.

Back at the car park, Emma was fastening her seatbelt when she saw Jed Riley climbing into an old van patched with rust.

'Jed doesn't seem to be doing very well for himself,' John observed as they drove back to Park Hall. 'A pity he threw away his chances at school.'

2

Emma woke the next morning with a rare feeling of freedom. For most of her life her daily timetable had been dictated by school, by college, by the need to look after her father. Now, for a short time until the impending financial crisis broke, she could do what she liked, and what she chose to do that morning was to garden.

Most of the five acres of land belonging to Park Hall was woodland or had reverted to scrub, brambles and nettles, but for the past eighteen months she had spent most of her limited free time in the walled flower garden, pruning the neglected roses and weeding around the self-sown flowers, and she prided herself that the results of her labours were beginning to show.

At lunchtime she went indoors and heated some soup in the gloomy semi-basement of a kitchen. It was dominated by an enormous table where cooks and kitchen maids had once toiled to feed the Digby family, but now only one end was in use where a small gas oven and a refrigerator had been fitted in near the sink.

Just then the telephone rang. George Stanford would like her to call and see him the following morning. He was polite, but the message was clear.

'The sooner you know all the details, the better,' he said ominously.

She agreed to the meeting and went back to digging vigorously, using the physical activity to stop her worrying about the future. An hour later, however, a shadow fell across the flowerbed she was tending, and she looked up to find John Burroughs smiling down at her. She stood up, aware of the fact that she was blushing, and tried to brush the soil from her hands while apologising for her unkempt state.

'You look fine,' he assured her.

She made the ritual offer of a cup of tea, but he shook his head.

'I only called in for a few minutes to see how you were. Yesterday must have been an ordeal for you, though you managed very well.'

Compliments and sympathy won him a smile, which he failed to notice as he was gazing over the grounds.

'Do you have to cope with all this? How much land is there?'

'There are five acres altogether, though everything except the flower garden here has been left to run wild since my father fell ill.'

He studied the landscape. 'It's all fairly flat, isn't it? Have you got a lake?'

'Not even a pond,' she said regretfully.

'Sometimes that can be a good thing,' he said enigmatically, and turned his attention to her once more. 'Incidentally, I dug out Jed Riley's mobile number last night and called him. I thought that as he is in the area he could call in to see if there are any antiques which you would be willing to part with.'

Emma felt a spark of anger. Although she had wondered about getting Mr Riley to look at the furniture, John had made the suggestion only yesterday, and already he had arranged for her belongings, not his, to be inspected with a view to selling them. Her feelings must have shown, for he said hastily, 'I can always call him and cancel the arrangement if you don't like the idea.'

She relaxed. He might have been over-hasty, but he had acted out of concern for her so he could be forgiven. The smile reappeared.

'It might be sensible to get a preliminary opinion and then I can decide what to do. I am going to see your uncle again in the morning, so it would be convenient if you could arrange for Mr Riley to call here about two o'clock tomorrow afternoon.'

As she walked with him towards his car, he looked up at the house as they passed in front of it. 'It's a sizeable place. Is it listed?'

'You mean listed by English Heritage? I'm afraid not. It is just an ordinary Victorian house, though there were probably older buildings on the same site before it.'

She waved goodbye as he drove away and went into the house feeling much happier.

The interview the following morning left her devastated, however. 'My father owed how much? But how could he? Where has all the money gone?'

George Stanford sighed, as if the foolishness of men with money never ceased to amaze him.

'When his income from investments fell and the cost of maintaining Park Hall grew, your father refused to change his lifestyle. For several years he was living on his capital, not his income. When he realised how little he had left, he tried to remedy the situation.' He sighed again, even more heavily. 'I've found out that he started gambling.'

Emma looked at him, trying to make sense of what he was saying. 'He bet on horses most of the time, but rarely managed to pick a winner. Did you have any idea of that?'

She shook her head slowly. 'I know he was always watching racing on television, but I thought that was just for amusement.' She looked at him with sudden alertness. 'He was always on the telephone. Was that how he placed his bets? I thought he was calling people he knew or dealing with his business affairs.'

'He always paid his bookmakers and the telephone bill, but that was about all.'

She was growing worried. 'Does that mean that debt collectors are going to start arriving? Will I lose my home?'

He leaned forward comfortingly. 'Nothing so dramatic. The people to whom he owned money aren't going to rush into action immediately. With your permission, I shall contact them and explain the situation. I'm sure they will wait when I tell them that you will eventually be able to pay the bills in full.'

She blinked. Where did he think the money was going to come from? 'How am I going to do that?'

'By selling Park Hall. It's the only thing you can do.'

His voice was calm and sensible, and after he had pointed out details of what was owing, she was forced to admit that of course it was the obvious thing to do. Even if her father had left her a fortune, Park Hall was far too big for a single woman.

She promised to think about what he had said and to inform him as soon as she had made up her mind, then picked up her handbag and took her leave.

George Stanford's last words were, 'And don't worry about our bill. We can wait.'

Emma walked home briskly, as though trying to outdistance her thoughts. Once there, she changed out of the neat suit she had thought suitable for the meeting with the solicitor and put on jeans and a sweater suitable for the garden. But instead of going outside, she sat brooding in the dismal kitchen.

She could not remember her mother, and Roger Digby had destroyed all pictures of his faithless wife and had never spoken of her to his daughter. When Emma had come home for the holidays, it was often to find that her father was absent on business or visiting acquaintances elsewhere. Park Hall itself, however, had always welcomed her. She had loved the house and the garden. It was her refuge and she was happy there.

Now it seemed inevitable that she must leave it. She would survive, of course. Emma knew herself to be intelligent and competent, able to carve out a career for herself, but she would miss Park Hall for the rest of her life.

She was disturbed by a knock at the door, and when she opened it, she was surprised to see Jed Riley standing there. This must have shown, for his grin faltered and he stepped back.

'Have I got the wrong time or the wrong day? John said you would expect me about two.'

'Oh, I'm sorry!' she exclaimed, remembering the arrangements made the previous day. 'I was expecting you now, it was just that I'd forgotten.' She held the door open. 'Please come in. I was just going to make a cup of tea.'

She led the way to the kitchen where Jed Riley looked round with such obvious disapproval that she felt the need to defend herself.

'I've been too busy to do much cleaning recently.'

He gave a definitely disapproving sniff. 'It looks to me as if this place hasn't been properly cleaned for a long time. My mum would be itching to give it a proper clear out.'

'Well, I should have more time to see to it now,' she snapped, plugging the electric kettle in. If Jed Riley spent his time doing house clearances he must have seen worse. He was supposed to be impressed by the size of the kitchen, not criticising her housework!

At that moment there was a sharp crack and a vicious blue spark leaped from the wall socket. The light on the kettle went out. It was the last straw.

'Now the kettle's broken! Everything is going wrong!'

Jed Riley unplugged the kettle and examined it. 'Where do you keep your fuses?' he enquired.

There was a small cupboard in a corner of the kitchen which held some basic tools, and when Emma scrabbled through them she was relieved to find a card of fuses. He took them from her, picked out a small screwdriver and set to work.

In a couple of minutes the kettle was plugged in again and was soon boiling, so that Emma was finally able to make a pot of tea. She thanked Jed for mending the kettle, but he brushed her thanks aside.

'I'm surprised it hasn't happened

before. The plug's wiring was loose. You could have been electrocuted.'

There was disapproval in his voice again, and when he had finished his tea, he stood up and started restlessly prowling around the kitchen.

'Now, do you want me to look at the furniture, or shall I come back another time?'

'Please, I'd like you to look now. I need to know whether there is anything worth selling before I put the house itself on the market.' She forced a smile. 'Perhaps you'll find something valuable.'

She led him into the hall, decorated with plaques showing groups of chubby cherubs. Together they went into the various ground floor rooms and then up the wide staircase to the bedrooms and finally to the attics where maidservants had once slept under the sloping roof.

Now as she opened door after door, she realised how neglected the rooms were, and how bare and unwelcoming they looked with the bedsteads stripped of mattresses and a layer of dust over everything. Jed Riley went round in silence, occasionally making a note on a small pad.

She opened the door to her own bedroom, but he simply stood in the doorway, gave a quick look round, shook his head and closed the door. Her father's bedroom still had the atmosphere of a sick room with medicine bottles and pillboxes lined up on a marble washstand, the television facing the bed and a telephone handy on the bedside table.

'My father was bedridden for well over a year,' she told Jed Riley as he inspected a small table, and he raised an eyebrow.

'I didn't know that.'

She noticed that his Liverpool accent had almost vanished.

Finally the tour was finished and they went back to the kitchen and once again sat down. He looked at his notes, frowning for some time and then spoke abruptly.

'When was the other furniture sold?'

'What other furniture?'

He shifted impatiently. 'Come on, Miss Digby, I'm not a fool. Someone has already been through this house, particularly the bedrooms, then stripped it of most of the good stuff. The small tables and cabinets that sell well, the ornaments, the kind of thing you would expect to find in a house like this, have all gone. What's left looks as though it has been brought down from the maids' bedrooms.

'The rugs have gone, and there are bare bulbs in some rooms where there should be light fittings. I've taken the time to come here because John Burroughs said it would be worth my while, but all I've seen is junk.'

Emma had had enough. Desperately she wanted to be on her own so that she could absorb this new blow. She stood up, supporting herself with one hand on the table because her knees felt suddenly weak.

'I'm sorry you are disappointed,' she

said coldly. 'I won't waste any more of your time.'

But instead of obediently moving towards the door, he came towards her. Suddenly his arm was round her shoulders guiding her to a chair.

'Sit down,' he ordered. It was easier to obey than protest, and she watched as he rapidly made another pot of tea, extracted the milk from the fridge and looked through the cupboards until he found a couple of clean mugs and a bag of sugar. He stirred a large spoonful into her mug and gave it to Emma. She shook her head.

'I don't take sugar.'

'You do today. You need it. I don't know what's the matter, but you look as if you are about to collapse,' he said firmly, and she took the mug obediently while he sat opposite her frowning, and watched her drink.

'What's going on? Didn't you know about the furniture?'

She leaned back in her chair and closed her eyes. 'I'm sorry to have been so dramatic, but your bad news was the final straw. You probably think me very unobservant, but I've been nursing my father since I came home eighteen months ago, and that was a full-time job so I didn't have time to go in most of the rooms, let alone check on the furniture.

'I think I know what must have happened to it though. My father must have sold it before he fell ill and I returned. He probably thought it wouldn't be noticed if stuff went from the bedrooms.'

'Any reason that you can think of?'

'My solicitor told me this morning that my father gambled away the last of his money and died in debt. That is why I've got to sell this house.'

'You didn't know till this morning? You poor girl!'

The unexpected pity made her eyes sting with tears. She shut them and heard him leave the room, to return a minute later.

'Here,' he said. 'I suspect you didn't

31

have any lunch. You can have half of these. They're cheese and pickle.'

She opened her eyes to find that he was dividing a bagful of sandwiches neatly between two plates, and suddenly she felt very hungry. After he had refilled their mugs and they had consumed the sandwiches to the last crumb, Jed Riley piled the mugs and plates neatly in the sink and returned to his seat.

'I owe you an apology,' he told her. 'I thought you came home just to bury your father and then turn everything he'd left into cash as soon as you could.'

'You also thought I was a rotten housekeeper,' she said with a flash of spirit, and he grinned.

'Well, I've certainly seen better. But it appears that the truth is that you've been too busy nursing your father for a long time to worry about anything else. I also get the impression that you don't really want to sell this house.'

'I don't,' she said with feeling, 'but

I've got no option. The trouble is that I was hoping that if I sold some furniture, I could get enough money to pay a few bills and have enough left to keep me going until the house is sold.'

He leaned back and stretched out his long legs. 'So it's that bad? Well, as I said, if there was any good stuff, it has already gone. But I might find enough bits and pieces to raise a couple of hundred if that would be any use.'

'Yes, please! It will all have to be cleared out soon, anyway, when the house goes.'

'Then we'll stop looking for antiques and start looking for the kind of thing that people might buy to use. You seem to have quite a nice dinner service in that cupboard, for example. Do you want to keep it?'

'I can't imagine myself giving dinner parties in the near future. Let's look through all the cupboards and then go back upstairs.'

It took another couple of hours, but finally Jed Riley had a list of china and furniture which he thought could be disposed of.

'I'll come to collect it tomorrow,' he told her. 'I'll bring some boxes and plenty of wrapping paper for the breakables. Remember, you'll have to pay the auction house a commission, and I take ten per cent. In your case, I'll calculate it on what's left after the auction people have taken their cut.'

'Anything is better than nothing, but will it all go in that little van?' she worried.

'I've got a lorry that I use for moving the tents,' he told her.

'Tents?'

'You know, marquees and things like that. I move them around from place to place.'

'Oh! I thought you just did house clearances and antiques.'

He had a peculiar expression on his face. 'Did John Burroughs tell you that?'

'Not in so many words. I must have got the wrong impression.' She looked at him with frank curiosity. 'He said you went to his school, but you left early. Why did you do that?'

His face went carefully blank. 'There were reasons.'

He was obviously not prepared to add to this curt statement and left soon afterwards.

'Thank you for your help, and for the sandwiches,' she said politely, and then added, 'I suppose you think I ought to go back in and start scrubbing the kitchen now?'

He gave a wicked grin. 'My mum would.'

3

Emma ignored the cobwebs and spent the evening with documents spread out over the big kitchen table. Calculator at the ready, she worked out how much money was owing and how much she had available. The largest amount owing was the mortgage which her father had taken out, his last opportunity to raise a large sum, which he had soon dissipated.

Set out in two neat tables, the results were definitely depressing, but there was one thing to be thankful for. Right up to the end her father had paid a small allowance into her bank account every three months. This was one reason why she had not suspected how short of money he was.

Perhaps she should have felt guilty, felt that the money rightfully belonged to one of the estate's creditors, but at least she would be able to eat. Surely none of the creditors would begrudge her that!

Jed Riley arrived at mid-morning in a lorry almost as battered as his van, accompanied by a little old man with the wrinkled face of a monkey who looked as if he should have been spending his declining years in an armchair, but who nevertheless heaved tables and chairs about with nonchalant ease.

The lorry was half-full when everything was packed, and Emma felt optimistically sure that it would bring a worthwhile amount.

'I'll let you know when the things are coming up for auction,' Jed promised, leaning out of the cab window, and then scowled as a car drove up the drive, blocking his way. The driver managed to squeeze his car alongside the lorry and got out. It was John Burroughs, and he stared at the lorry, then recognised the man in the cab.

'Jed Riley! So you've come to look at the furniture.'

'I've come to take it away — or what's left, so will you please get out of the way?' Jed responded, and then waved goodbye to Emma and drove off without saying anything more when the car had been moved.

Emma invited John into the house. It had seemed natural to take Jed Riley into the kitchen, but somehow that did not seem appropriate for John, so instead she led him into the morning-room, still bathed in sunshine, and pulled the dustcovers off a pair of chairs.

'I wanted to see how you were,' he said, smiling down at her before he took a seat. 'Sometimes people find themselves getting depressed a few days after the funeral when the pressure is off and there is not enough to keep them occupied.'

It was pleasant to feel that someone was concerned about her, but she reassured him. 'You needn't worry about me. I've been very busy. Jed called yesterday and went through the house. Unfortunately he didn't find anything valuable, but he is taking some things to auction.'

'Did he leave you a list, or give you a receipt?'

She had never thought of asking for either, and John shook his head when she told him this.

'Jed Riley lives on his wits, wheeling and dealing. I'm not saying he would take advantage of you, but I suppose there is the possibility that one or two pieces could vanish somewhere between here and the auction house.'

'I am sure I can trust him. He was very kind,' she said frostily.

'I hope you are right.'

There was an awkward silence, broken when John took a file from the briefcase he was carrying. 'My uncle said that he had had to give you bad news, so I took the liberty of looking up one or two firms which deal with the sale of large properties like Park Hall.

This one looks the most promising.'

'Can't that wait a few weeks? I realise I will have to sell Park Hall eventually, but I would like to enjoy it for a little while by myself before possible buyers start tramping through it.'

'I appreciate that you don't want to give up your home, but I think the sooner you start organising the sale the better. You need advice on the price you should ask, and where it should be advertised. Anyway, buyers won't be very interested in the house. They'll be more interested in the grounds.'

'But if they are hoping to live in this house of course they'll want to inspect it.'

'Live in it?'

He sounded surprised, as though the idea had never occurred to him, and she looked at him patiently.

'What else are they going to do with it?'

'Knock it down and build houses on the land.'

She felt as if she had been physically

punched in the stomach. John saw her consternation but obviously could not understand it.

'What did you think was going to happen to it?'

'I thought a family would buy it, or perhaps it could be turned into a hotel.'

He shook his head slowly. 'Emma, it would cost a fortune to do this house up or convert it. I know you are fond of it because it has been your family's home, but even you must admit it isn't particularly beautiful or desirable. But it has tremendous value as building land. With five acres there is room to build at least fifty houses.'

'You don't understand! It was bad enough when I realised I had to leave my home, but to think of it being knocked down, reduced to a pile of rubble so that dozens of little houses can be put on the park - that's much worse!'

He looked at her reproachfully. 'Worse? What is worse than an old house being demolished is the thought of all the people who want houses, somewhere decent to bring up their families, but who can't find anything to buy in the place where they want to live.'

'But my home will be gone!'

'You won't be here. You'll have the memory of Park Hall, but the fact that the actual building no longer exists won't make any difference to you.

'Emma, it will take weeks to sort everything out, and I want to help you get the best deal possible. You can wait a while before actually putting it up for sale, but at least let me apply on your behalf for outline planning permission to build houses. If you have that permission it will add to the value of the estate.'

His patience made her feel like a sulky child trying to put off the inevitable.

'Oh, go ahead. Try and get the planning permission.'

When he drove away a little later there was a satisfied smile on his face.

Emma was not prepared to let Park Hall vanish without a fight, however. During the next few days she was in constant contact with various national organisations, only to find that although everybody was in favour of preserving open spaces and the national heritage, nobody wanted a dilapidated Victorian mansion with a few acres unless it came with a large amount of money for its upkeep.

'I don't want anything for myself,' she explained to one man. 'You'd just have to pay off the mortgage.'

'Not a chance,' came the frank answer. 'We have plenty of famous and beautiful buildings that are crying out for attention. I wish you well, but I think you are fighting a losing battle.'

Her last hope was the local town council and she made an appointment to see the mayor. She explained her offer once again.

'All you would have to pay is the mortgage, and I'm sure that is a lot less than the value of the estate.'

For once she appeared to have a receptive listener. The mayor's eyes were gleaming. 'And for that we would get the house and the land?'

'All of it.'

He scribbled a few notes. 'I must admit we could do with the space. The house might be useful for our offices, and we've been looking for somewhere to build council houses.'

'No! I would sell you the estate cheaply on condition the grounds became a public park.'

The mayor flung his pencil down. 'That's out of the question! Do you know how much it costs to keep up open spaces?'

'Then I withdraw my offer!'

They glared at each other. 'I am sorry you aren't prepared to be more public-spirited,' the mayor said frostily.

'I'm prepared to give the town a park to enjoy, but not another housing estate,' Emma said firmly.

The mayor half-rose, as if to usher her out, but then an idea seemed to occur to him and he sank down into his chair again.

'If you want to give the townspeople a chance to enjoy your gardens, there is something you could do. It's the annual town fete soon. Years ago, of course, it was always held in the grounds of Park Hall, but your father stopped that and we started to use the playing field at the local secondary school. We were going to do that again, but the headmaster called this morning to say that they are going to hold a cricket tournament there and he can't risk the turf being ruined by stalls and hundreds of people milling around.

'Could we hold it in the grounds of Park Hall? From what you say, this is probably the last year that the Digby family could play host to the fete.'

It seemed a harmless request, and would give Emma a chance to do one last good deed for the town where her family had lived for so long.

'I don't see why not,' she said pensively. 'But the lawns are very overgrown.'

'Don't worry about that,' the mayor said briskly. 'We'll send in the council groundsmen to mow and generally tidy up. It won't cost you a penny.'

But Emma was beginning to think of difficulties. 'What about insurance? And toilets?'

'The town council will see to the insurance, and we always arrange for temporary toilets,' he promised her, and now he was rising to show her out. 'I'll let you have all the details of what's involved, but you won't have to do anything, Miss Digby.'

It sounded very reassuring, but Emma soon began to question the statement. First of all big mowers swept away the long grass and bramble, and then telephone calls came from people anxious to measure the park and decide where various activities should be allocated. Then it appeared that the provision of refreshments would need access to water and electricity.

Emma resisted a suggestion that the caterers should take over her kitchen, but finally agreed that they should be accommodated in the old stable block, long since converted to a garage.

A squad of women arrived to clean and scrub the garage and were constantly knocking on the door to ask for more hot water, the loan of a bucket, or permission to use her toilet. It finally dawned on Emma that it was curiosity as much as any real need that motivated most of these calls. Few of the townspeople had ever been in or ever near the big house on the edge of town.

As large banners throughout the town announced the new venue for the fete, Emma began to fear that she would be under virtual siege on the actual day.

'I wish I'd never agreed to have the fete here,' she complained to John Burroughs. 'If it's like this now, what is it going to be like on the actual day?'

They were sitting in the morning-room, which she had cleaned and polished till it was a comfortable little sitting-room. John had got into the habit of dropping in when he was in the area with the excuse that he just wanted to check that she was all right.

'Now he gave a lazy smile. 'You'll love it. As lady of the manor you'd better wear a pretty frock and a big hat. I'm just sorry I can't be here for long.'

'You can forget the frock and the hat, anyway. I've spent most of my life away from the town. Very few people will even know who I am.'

The fete did not open officially till ten o'clock, but the organisers were busy there at seven and the stallholders started to arrive soon afterwards. Emma, enjoying a late cup of coffee before she ventured out, nearly dropped her cup when she saw someone bending down to peer through the kitchen window.

The actual fete was colourful, noisy, and full of people enjoying themselves. Sunny weather had brought the crowds flocking to the park. With John by her side, Emma wandered among them, telling herself that she was enjoying it all, but mentally uneasy at having her quiet private place invaded by all these strangers. She was furious when she found one family happily picking bunches of flowers from her cherished garden and they were very reluctant to believe that she had any right to tell them to stop.

John was the first to see Jed Riley, looking scruffier than ever, rummaging among the bric-a-brac.

'What's he doing here?' he said with obvious dislike.

Jed greeted them casually. 'I saw the sign as I was driving through, so I thought I'd drop in. You never know what you'll find on these stalls.'

'And if you find anything worthwhile you won't tell the stallholder what it's really worth,' John said disapprovingly.

'Certainly not. I've got to make a living. Now, excuse me, I've still got a couple of stalls to inspect.'

John's gaze followed him. 'He had a chance to make something of his life and he threw it away,' he commented, and then turned to Emma. 'I'm afraid I'll have to go now. I have to be in Liverpool in thirty minutes.'

She watched his car drive away and then returned to the fete, but her heart sank when she was accosted by one of the few people she recognised. Mrs Anthea Fernley had hoped to become the second Mrs Digby before she accepted the late Mr Fernley, and was inclined to behave as if the wish to become Emma's stepmother had given her the right to behave as if there was some connection between them. She was expensively dressed, perfectly and heavily made up, and every hair was in its appointed place.

'There you are, Emma, our hostess for the day.' She looked at Emma's old jeans and T-shirt with obvious pity. 'I must say, you haven't really tried to dress the part, have you? But then, you haven't had much time to spend on yourself.' She lowered her voice. 'Of course, you saw the flowers I sent to your father's funeral. I am planning to call on you soon, my dear. Now you are on your own you will need guidance on who you should get to know, and what you should get involved in. I can help you there.'

She wandered away before Emma could think of a suitable reply, and she was left wondering why Mrs Fernley had never called to offer any help during the past months when she had really needed it. Perhaps it was because she had known that Roger Digby detested her and would have ordered Emma to keep her out of the house.

Emma decided she had had enough, but on her way back to the house was stopped by another woman, this one looking very earnest and determined.

'Miss Digby, I want a word with you. I'm Susan Shelley, and I'm one of the people who care about the environment in this town. It is true you are planning to sell Park Hall as building land?'

'Probably,' Emma asked briefly, resisting the urge to ask what business it was of Susan Shelley's.

'But you mustn't do that! The house and park are an important part of the history of this town. It is your duty to preserve them.'

Emma's lips tightened. 'Unfortunately, I am afraid I can't do that, much as I would like to do so.'

The woman's face turned red and she seemed to swell physically. 'That's nonsense! Everybody knows that the Digby family have always had plenty of money. You're just being greedy, selling the place for what you can get because you don't care about it.'

Emma brushed past her, too furious to speak. If only the woman knew the truth!

She returned to the house, determined to stay in her bedroom where no-one could peer through the windows till the fete was over. The back door was unlocked, and she scolded herself for her carelessness, but a quick look round the basement and ground floor did not reveal any intruders. But halfway up the first flight of stairs she stopped. She could hear footsteps above.

Emma hesitated, wondering whether she should go for help, but decided that it would take too long to find anyone useful and explain what was the matter. Taking a deep breath, she climbed the stairs swiftly, started towards the bedrooms and saw an elderly woman in a shapeless tweed coat opening a door and peering into the room beyond.

'Can I help you?' Emily said icily.

The woman turned and looked at her with no sign of guilt. 'I'm looking for a toilet,' she announced.

'You'll find them on the field.'

'I'm not using those,' the woman said scornfully. 'I don't feel safe in them.'

Emma felt that she should order her out of the house, but the woman looked respectable enough and was not carrying a bag in which she could have hidden any small objects she had taken a liking to. Besides, Emma could sympathise with her dislike of the temporary toilets.

'There is a bathroom here,' she indicated, and waited outside till the woman reappeared and then ushered her downstairs and out through the kitchen. The woman took her time, not trying to conceal the fact that she was inspecting everything and Emma saw her give a disdainful look at the antiquated kitchen equipment. When they reached the back door the woman turned to Emma.

'You should have shown me straight out when you found me,' she said briskly. 'You're too polite and you're too trusting. You should have insisted on looking in my handbag as well. Make sure you lock the door now. Oh, and thank you for letting me use your toilet.'

She stumped away, leaving Emma torn between annoyance and amusement. However she followed her advice and locked the door and then retreated upstairs with some sandwiches and fruit only venturing out again at four o'clock when most of the stallholders had packed and gone.

She walked out on to the lawns and then stopped, horrified. The surface of the grass was scored with car tracks and holes showed where stallholders had hammered posts into the ground. The organisers had provided a skip for rubbish, but abandoned litter marked too many sites and napkins which had held burgers and hot dogs were blowing across the lawns.

Two organisers were standing chatting and she hurried up to them, demanding to know when the mess would be cleared up. They showed no wish to spring into action.

'There's always a few who don't clear up after them,' one said resignedly. 'I'll see if I can get a couple of the lads to come round sometime tomorrow and tidy the place up a bit. You can't expect us to do anything now. We've been busy since seven o'clock, remember.'

Defeated, Emma retreated to her

bedroom again and watched as the grounds emptied of the few remaining figures. The day had fulfilled her worst fears.

4

There was a loud repeated knock on the front door and Emma hurried to open it. Perhaps John Burroughs had found an opportunity to call back after all, and she looked forward to telling him her woes and enjoying his sympathy. But when she opened the door it was Jed Riley who stood there.

'Oh! What do you want? I thought you went hours ago.'

'Thank you for the warm welcome,' he returned strolling past her into the house, and she was forced to follow him down to the kitchen.

'What I want first,' he said, reaching for the kettle as if it were his own kitchen, 'is a cup of tea. I left here soon after I saw you, and I've had a very busy day. After that, I'll help you clean up after the fete.'

He drew a small plastic bag out of his

pocket, extracted two teabags and dropped them into the teapot. 'Yorkshire tea,' he informed her. 'I prefer it.'

She was torn between irritation at his behaviour and gratitude for his unexpected offer of help, and settled on accepting a cup of tea from him.

'How did you know I might need help?'

'I've dismantled enough tents after affairs like that to know what the place is like afterwards.'

Out in the park he surveyed the scene and issued instructions.

'Right, well I assume you've got a wheelbarrow? I'll put all the metal, plastic and glass rubbish in the tip. We'll make a pile of wood and anything else that will burn safely and we'll have a bonfire. You can collect all this paper blowing around in a bin bag.'

He picked up a large empty cardboard box which one stallholder had abandoned. 'We'll need this for the items that people will come looking for tomorrow. You'll be surprised what they lose — spectacles, jackets, cameras, even handbags.'

An hour later the lawns were not spotless but there was a great improvement. A bonfire was cheerfully consuming a lot of the rubbish and the cardboard box was nearly full of personal items which their owners would be glad to recover. Emma felt tired, sweaty and dirty, but the physical exercise and sense of achievement had lightened her mood.

'That's all we can do. The light will be going soon, anyway.'

Jed strode over to his old van, leant inside, and retrieved a large carrier bag. 'This is our reward for our hard work. It's a full Chinese takeaway for two, and it won't take long to heat it up.'

Back in the kitchen, efficiently unpacking the various foil containers, Jed became aware of Emma's critical gaze. 'What's the matter?'

'I don't know how to put this nicely, but do you realise what a bully you are? You haven't stopped ordering me about since I opened the door.'

He stood still for a few seconds, and then carefully placed another foil container on a baking tray.

'But you did what I told you. Why?'

'Because what you said seemed a good — a reasonable — idea.'

'Exactly!' he said triumphantly. 'So what was the point in wasting time in making suggestions and discussing what to do if I was right all along? I don't like wasting time.'

'Aren't you possibly a bit over-confident?'

'You mean big-headed?'

'Yes!'

He grinned happily. 'I've been earning my own living for a long time, Emma Digby. One of the first lessons I learnt was that I had to convince people that I knew what I was doing. Quite often I was bluffing, but nowadays I usually know what I'm talking about, though my mum still only has to take one look at me and she knows when I'm lying.'

As they ate the takeaway, Emma told him about the fete, including the elderly lady she had found in the house. 'And she told me off for giving her the chance to snoop around!'

'She was right,' he commented. 'I hope you check the doors and windows at night. By the way, the kitchen is looking a bit better. Have you been having a clean-up?'

'Thank you. I thought I might as well do something, even if I don't know how long I'll be here to enjoy it. I have been working on the kitchen, and I've gone through a couple of other rooms. John says the morning-room is looking very good.'

'John Burroughs? Well, he's got a lot more polish than I have. He wouldn't order you around.'

They finished the meal and Emma cleared away the plates while Jed piled the foil containers back in the carrier bag.

'One reason I called is that the stuff I took from here is coming up for auction in a week's time,' Jed said. 'I took it to Harburton's. It's a general sale, not a fine arts sale. Would you like to come along and see how much you get?'

Emma confessed that she had never been to an auction and was curious to see what actually happened.

'Good. I'll meet you there about eleven. It's viewing in the morning, then we can get something to eat, and the auction starts at two o'clock.'

John Burroughs called the next day, full of apologies for not being able to stay at the fete, but she told him there would have been little he could do.

'The place was left in rather a mess, but Jed Riley helped me clear up. He wanted to invite me to see my furniture auctioned next week.'

'That might be a good idea,' John said thoughtfully. 'You haven't got a list of what he took, remember. If you are at the auction you will probably notice if any major items are missing.'

'I've told you, I trust him!'

'I'm only trying to protect you,' he

said stiffly, and she apologised.

'I know, and I'm grateful. How is the planning application coming along?'

'No news yet, but I'm keeping in touch. Incidentally, I know how much you hate the idea, but I think you should ask those developers I mentioned to come and have a preliminary look round. You need not commit yourself definitely, and neither will they, but they might give you an idea of how much they would offer.'

Emma felt that it was probably remorse for her previous short temper that made her agree. Before he left John suggested that he called after she got back from the auction so that she could tell him all the details.

Someone rang from the developers the very next day. Either they were very eager to buy Park Hall, or John Burroughs had been in touch with them before he spoke to her. The following day a large man appeared and spent a couple of hours carefully inspecting and measuring the grounds.

'There don't seem to be any drawbacks,' he announced. 'Having access to the road is useful, though it means some of the houses will suffer with traffic noise. At least there are no steep slopes and no water to deal with.' Emma was reminded of John's comments. 'You're sure the grounds and the house aren't on any list of places to be preserved?'

'Unfortunately not. Apparently they are just not special enough.'

'We like it like that. Now, if you don't mind, I'd like to look round the house.'

'I was told you would just knock it down.'

'Probably. But there is a market for apartments, and some people might like to have Park Hall as their address.'

She felt a small flicker of hope, and after his inspection she anxiously asked him his opinion.

'It's not up to me to decide, but I think the basic structure is sound, and it could be converted into flats. You've got a good-looking entrance hall.

People would like that, so we would try to keep it, but it would be easier to gut the rest and just keep the façade.'

* * *

The visitor who called two days later was totally unexpected. Emma opened the door in response to a knock to find a grey-haired woman standing outside.

She was dressed in a neat grey coat and clutching a large handbag. When the door opened she stood and looked at Emma without speaking.

'Can I help you?' Emma enquired. 'I'm Emma Digby.'

'I know you are,' the woman replied. 'You were named after me. I'm Emma Jennings, your grandmother – your mother's mother.'

Emma stared at her in amazement.

'Do you want proof?' the woman challenged her. 'I've got letters, a photograph of my daughter's wedding. You look just like her when she was your age.'

65

But that was unnecessary. The outline of her face, the shape of the cheekbones, were familiar to Emma from her own reflection in the mirror.

'Come in,' she said quietly, and led her grandmother to the morning room.

Emma escaped to the kitchen to prepare a tea tray. Her mind was a confusion of different emotions. Although she could recall virtually nothing of her mother, she could still remember the feeling of loss when she had disappeared.

The little Emma had gathered over the following years from Roger Digby had portrayed her as a faithless wife and unloving mother, but the absence of hard fact had secretly allowed Emma to create a mental picture of a lovely woman who would return one day to rescue her daughter from her lonely life and take her away to some exotic new home.

That dream had faded as the years passed, until she rarely thought of that other parent. Now excitement stirred.

Had her grandmother come as a forerunner of her daughter? Would Emma finally meet her mother again?

She carried the tray up to the morning room and found Mrs Jennings still sitting as she had left her, her bag clasped in both hands.

'How much do you know about Amy?' Mrs Jennings asked suddenly.

'Nothing. My father never spoke of her and destroyed any trace of her.'

Mrs Jenning's face hardened. 'Well, I didn't approve of her leaving her husband and child, but there were faults on both sides and I could understand why she did it.' She put her cup down carefully and sat bolt upright, as if nerving herself to perform an unpleasant duty. 'Your mother's dead. After Ronaldo left her she went to America. Then she met a man called Walter Buchan in Florida and married him. They didn't have any children, so you needn't worry that any half-brothers or half-sisters are going to turn up.'

She gave the information briskly, and then looked at Emma interrogatively. 'Have you got any questions?'

Emma was as blunt as her grandmother. 'Yes. Why are you here?'

Mrs Jennings looked down and fumbled with the handles of her bag.

'To see you,' she said finally. 'You are my grandchild, my flesh and blood.'

'Why now?'

'A friend of mine who lives in Liverpool called me and told me that your father was dead. I knew he'd never let me in this house while he lived, but I thought that with him gone there would be a chance to meet you.'

'You mean that suddenly after fifteen years you decided to take an interest in me?'

Mrs Jennings looked at her with deep hurt in her eyes. 'That's not true! After Amy ran away your father wouldn't let me see you. But every birthday, every Christmas, I've sent you a card, and each time I've written my name and address in it. I hoped the time would come when you would reply, but you never did. Amy used to ask if I had any news of you, and there was never anything to tell her.'

'I didn't know that! I never saw any of those cards! I was away at boarding school each year when it was my birthday.'

The two looked at each other, and gradually Mrs Jennings gave a shaky smile. 'It looks as though we've a lot to tell each other. Shall I start?'

In the next hour Emma learnt that she had an uncle, Simon, who had two sons, and that they lived in Surrey, while Mrs Jennings herself still lived in the house in Fulham where she had brought up her family and had stayed on after her children had grown up and gone and her husband had died. From her bag she proudly produced photographs of Simon and her grandchildren.

'He doesn't know I've come here,' she confided. 'He thought it would be best to forget all about the Digbys. You wait till I tell him about you, though.

He'll want to meet you then.'

After a little hesitation, she brought out some more photographs which she spread on the table. 'These are of your mother.'

Emma gazed at them for some time. Her mother's face was the face of a stranger, quite unlike Emma's mental attempts to ignore her. She picked up one which showed a young Amy Jennings laughing and carefree, and wondered what her life would have been like if her mother had stayed with her.

'You can keep that if you like,' her grandmother offered, and Emma took it gratefully.

It did not take long to give an account of her own life, and she spent almost as much time explaining why she was now planning to sell the house.

'So Roger Digby got into trouble with his money, didn't tell anybody, and tried to get it back by gambling,' Mrs Jennings said thoughtfully. 'It sounds typical of Roger. He would never admit that he had any faults, and could never bring himself to ask for help. That was one of the reasons Amy left him.

'She married him because he was handsome, because she was impressed by the fact that he had a big house with lots of land where his family had lived for a long time. It was so very different from the way we lived in Fulham! But she got tired of being expected to treat him as if he was absolutely marvellous at everything, when she knew he was just an ordinary man who sometimes got himself into messes because he wouldn't take advice.'

'Why didn't she take me with her when she left him?' It was a question Emma had wanted to ask for fifteen years.

'I can't give you a simple answer, because I could never have left a child of mine and I didn't understand how she could. She knew your father adored you and would care for you. And of course she was madly in love with Ronaldo at the time and he would never have taken her with a child. That wouldn't have fitted in with his lifestyle at all!'

'Then he left her.'

'Yes, but by then I think she had fallen out of love with him as well. Anyway, Walter Buchan made her happy.'

She gathered the photographs up from the table and put them neatly away in her bag. 'Don't think too hardly of her.'

'I don't. She left me a long time ago. I have always been curious about her, and I'm glad that I now know what happened to her.'

They spent more time chatting to each other, gradually getting to know each other.

'Would you like to look round the place?' Emma suggested at one point, and showed her grandmother round the gardens and then the house. Mrs Jennings approved of the flower garden but the lawns and wooded areas did not attract her, and she shook her head after being shown round the house.

'It's too big,' she said firmly. 'I understand why you are so fond of it. It must have been a fine place in the days when there were plenty of servants, but it's quite unsuitable for you now.'

This time she accompanied Emma to the kitchen to help make another cup of tea, and it seemed natural for them to drink it sitting by the big kitchen table.

'What are you planning to do after the house is gone?' she asked.

'Well, I thought I could finish training to be a teacher. That will take another couple of years. Then I can decide where I want to live and look for a job.'

'What about boyfriends? Is there anyone you want to stay near?'

Emma laughed. 'No-one! I met some nice boys when I started training, but they were friends who were boys, not boyfriends.'

Mrs Jennings refused an invitation to stay the night, and told Emma that she would not see her the following day, as she was going back to London on an early train.

'My friend in Liverpool was glad to put me up for a couple of days so I could catch a train here, and I want to get back to her before it gets late.'

'You came all this way just to see me for a few hours?'

Mrs Jennings smiled. 'Well, your father always made it clear that he thought he had married beneath him. For all I knew, you might have felt the same.'

'You mean I might have been a snob?'

'Yes, and anyway I didn't want to overdo the first meeting. We've both got a lot to think about.'

'But we will see each other again?'

'London's got some good training colleges. I know it is a very expensive place to live, but it wouldn't be if you lived with me.'

Emma was taken aback, but her grandmother went on. 'I can't save your house for you, but I can give you somewhere else to live, and I think we would get on together reasonably well. Anyway, I'm your grandmother and it's my duty to help you.'

5

Harburton's Auction Rooms were on the outskirts of the local market town, where they held regular auctions. Occasionally they collected enough valuable furniture and paintings to hold a fine arts sale, but their general sales were most popular with the public. Here you could buy a tea set for a couple of pounds, a very miscellaneous box of oddments for ten, or a chest of drawers for fifteen.

Emma parked in the muddy area politely described as a car park and found Jed waiting for her at the door to the saleroom. He was chatting to a couple of men, but broke off and waved to Emma as she approached. The two men, dressed like Jed in jeans, heavy jackets and boots, were introduced as dealers. Emma, also in jeans and a jacket and without any make-up, decided she had chosen the right things to wear.

'Like me, these lads come to every little sale like this convinced they are going to find something worth a fortune and buy it for a tenner,' Jed said cheerfully, and the Liverpool accent was back, stronger than ever. The two guffawed, obviously on friendly terms with him, and went off as Jed took Emma by the arm and guided her inside.

The saleroom had brick walls and a high tin roof. Furniture of all kinds was lined up in rough rows on the floor, looking neglected and abandoned, and cardboard boxes full of smaller items covered trestle tables.

'What do you think of it?' Jed asked.

Emma hesitated, before deciding to be truthful. 'It looks — depressing.'

He grinned widely.

'Look again. It's treasure trove. This is where you come when you're trying to find a few plates to match your dinner service, or when you want a dining table and chairs and you can't afford the prices in the shiny new shops.' He indicated the furniture. 'That table may look a wreck to you, but someone is going to buy it, clean it up and polish it, and it will give them years of service.'

'If you say so,' she said doubtfully, and then stiffened. 'Look! Those chairs are mine.'

Recognising the items she had sent was a miserable process. The furniture looked dusty and unloved, and the items of china and kitchenware were piled up carelessly as though no-one thought them worth bothering about.

Then the sight of a brightly-painted Spanish jug in one box distracted her. She picked it up and examined it, put it back when she saw an ornate pair of scales, and moved on to a box full of china jugs of all shapes and colours.

'Now you're getting the idea,' Jed told her. 'Rummage! You don't know what you'll find.'

He himself was examining a battered

folio-size volume which he had pulled out from underneath rows of books in one box.

'What's that?'

'Cartoons, by the look of it,' he said briefly, pushing the volume back and looking at the titles of the other books.

By the time she had examined the array of cheap prints and amateur watercolours that hung on the walls he seemed to have lost interest in the boxes.

'Let's go and get something to eat,' he suggested, steering her towards the exit. Ten minutes' walk brought them to a shop front roughly painted bright red, with a hand-painted notice announcing in uneven letters that here they would find a self-service buffet.

There was already a queue of people serving themselves as Jed and Emma took a large plate each. The food was basic and solid, clearly meant to fill the customers up as cheaply as possible. Chips, sausages, fried eggs and baked beans were available in large quantities, as well as black pudding and fried bread.

Emma resigned herself to indigestion and started to fill her plate. As they waited to pay, Jed put his hand in his jeans pocket. A horrified look appeared on his face, and he turned to Emma urgently.

'I've left my wallet in the van! I've only got a five-pound note. Have you got some money?'

She searched her pockets anxiously. 'I've got ten pounds.'

'That means we are still a pound short. Oh, give me what you've got and I'll promise them to bring the extra money later.'

When their turn came to pay Emma was tense, waiting for an embarrassing and possibly humiliating confrontation.

'Twelve pounds,' said the cashier, giving them a bored look.

'How much?'

'Twelve pounds,' the girl repeated impatiently. 'One adult, one half price.'

Jed pocketed the change and was smiling widely as they sat down at a plastic-covered table. 'That was a stroke of luck.'

Emma was not so happy. 'I don't look like a child!'

'Don't get upset. In a few years' time you'll be glad if someone thinks you are younger than you really are.'

The food proved to be hot, freshly prepared and good, and she cleared her plate, but refused the treacle sponge and custard available, though Jed happily helped himself.

'Do you do anything else besides move tents and deal in antiques?' she asked him.

'I do whatever turns up, but it is mostly tents and antiques.'

'Which do you prefer?'

'The tents bring in steady money, but antiques are more fun.'

'How did you learn about them?'

'You mean how did someone as rough as me learn about artists and craftsmen?'

She did not reply, aware that deep down she had been wondering that very thing.

He leant back and stared over her head, as though looking back in time. 'John Burroughs told you I left his posh school instead of going on to do A-Levels. I didn't intend to. I had dreams of going on to university, of becoming a doctor or something like that, but then my father was killed in an accident in the Liverpool docks. He and Mum had bought a house just a couple of years before he died and it meant a lot to them to actually have a place that belonged to them after years of renting places.

'The school wanted me to stay on. There were grants, the possibility of loans, but there wouldn't have been enough to pay the mortgage. Mum would have had to go back to a council flat, and I knew that it would kill her to lose her home just after losing Dad. So I left school and Mum and I did whatever we could that would bring in a little money. Mum did cleaning and some sewing at home. I started the day delivering papers and then I ran errands for various people, helped on a fruit stall in the market, did a late shift at a general store.

'One week we had too many bills and not enough money, so I took a vase that Mum had bought in a jumble sale to an antique shop because I thought I'd seen something like it in a television programme. Anyway, after a lot of bargaining I persuaded the shop owner to give me fifteen pounds for it. Mum and I were both pleased as anything and I thought I'd done very well. Then I saw the vase in his window priced at £50! So I decided there was money in antiques if you knew what you were doing.

'I got books out of the library and spent what spare time I had in sale rooms. When I first went to sales I didn't buy anything. I watched what sold well and what didn't and I listened to the dealers talking to each other.

Now I'm not an expert, but I make a profit.'

'And did you keep the house?' Emma asked.

He looked at her with pride. 'We kept the house. The mortgage is paid off and we both live there, though Mum has started to tell me that it's time I got married and got my own home, but I tell her I haven't got time to find a girl.'

Here there was a discreet cough and they looked up to find a large man holding a full plate and looking significantly at their empty cups. The café had filled up for lunchtime and obviously other customers wanted their table.

'Just going,' Jed murmured, and they left the café and started to walk back to the auction rooms.

'It's a pity my father wasn't as practical when it came to saving our home,' sighed Emma.

'How do you feel about him?'

'At first, when Mr Stanford told me what he had done, I was very angry.

84

Now I feel sorry for him, especially since I talked to my grandmother.'

Jed halted. 'What grandmother? I thought you only had an aunt.'

Emma explained about the sudden appearance of her maternal grandmother. 'I liked her. And don't tell me she appeared so quickly after my father died because she thought she might get something out of me because her daughter was once married to my father! She wasn't like that!'

'The best confidence tricksters are the ones you trust on sight.'

'She knows I have nothing.'

'Except a great big chunk of possibly valuable building land.'

'I still trust her and if I do decide to finish teacher training I may take up her offer to go and live with her.' She struggled to put her feelings into words. 'Perhaps I want to trust her because I need to feel that I am linked to someone, that I'm not completely isolated.'

'Be careful. Don't trust someone just

because you want to. Remember, you have an aunt.'

'She would like to forget I exist.'

They found two dining-room chairs to sit on in the auction rooms. The auctioneer was obviously familiar with many of those waiting to bid, and spent a few minutes joking with them before the auction began. Emma was taken aback at the speed with which he conducted the sale.

Her own items were scattered through the afternoon. Some seemed to her to be going for very little, though the dinner service which had attracted Jed's attention went for fifty pounds, which he told her was an excellent price as he methodically noted down the successful bids.

'You'll be surprised how it adds up,' he reassured her.

When the box of books he had examined in the morning came up for sale, he was the only bidder.

'Eight pounds,' Emma said. 'Is it worth that?'

'Mum likes a good book to read, so she can sort through those and dump the ones she doesn't want.'

At the end of the afternoon he told her she would get just over three hundred pounds, after commission had been deducted.

'I can live on that for a while,' she said with relief. 'I can even send off a bit to some of the creditors.'

It was late afternoon when they finally left the saleroom.

'Would you like to come somewhere for a drink to celebrate?' Jed asked.

'Thank you, but I'd better get back to Park Hall. John Burroughs said he would call.'

'There's plenty of time for a drink. You don't have to rush back just to see him,' Jed said impatiently, but she insisted that she wanted to get back, so he walked beside her to her car.

'Thank you for all you've done,' she said gratefully. 'I have enjoyed today very much, as well as making a little money.'

'Glad to have helped,' he responded. 'Let me know if there is anything else I can do.'

'There is one thing.'

He lifted an enquiring eyebrow.

'Give me my six pounds!'

With a melodramatic sigh, Jed slowly counted out six one-pound coins into her hand and closed her fingers over them.

'Keep them safe. I may want to borrow them again sometime.'

She was still giggling as she drove away, and halfway home she pulled in a lay-by and phoned John Burroughs.

'Emma Digby here, ready to report on the day,' she said gaily when she heard his voice.

'Emma! I hope it was a good day. I'll see you at Park Hall in about half an hour then.'

'Actually, I'm not far from home now. I'll be there in about five minutes.'

'Five minutes?' There was a note of surprise. 'Well, I'll probably get there a bit later. See you then.'

It had been a good day, she reflected contentedly as she drove the last few miles. It had been profitable and instructive, but it had also been fun, something that had been missing from her life. Jed Riley had been a very good companion.

She swerved slightly as a lorry coming towards her at high speed appeared round a bend in the road and roared past her without slowing down. It looked old and uncared for, but there was no name on the dusty side.

Emma turned into Park Hall drive and came to a halt by the side of the house. There was just time probably to comb her hair and apply a little makeup. Jed Riley and his dealer friends might not care what she looked like, but she felt that John Burroughs would appreciate it if she looked as if she had made an effort with her appearance for him.

The first hint of trouble came when the back door swung open as she started to insert her key. When she looked, there were marks on the wood round the lock. It had been forced open. Emma took one step, then two, into the empty kitchen, looked round, and then fled outside. John Burroughs found her huddled on the front doorstep with her arms round her knees when he arrived five minutes later.

'What's the matter?' he demanded in alarm.

'Someone has broken in while I've been away. I dare not go in, because they might still be there.'

'Have you called the police?'

'I never thought of that. I was waiting for you.'

John's mobile phone appeared and he rapidly tapped away and then spoke to the police.

'They'll be here in a few minutes, and told us not to go in till they get here,' he reported, sitting down beside her on the step and putting his arm round her. 'Emma! You're shivering!'

'I'm not cold. It's just a nervous reaction.' Suddenly she turned and clung to him. 'I'm frightened, John! Why should anyone break in? There's nothing to take.'

'It was probably someone who broke in on impulse when they found the house was empty. I expect they are long gone.'

When a police car arrived, one policeman went into the house while his companion stayed with Emma to find out what had happened. By the time she had finished telling him the few details the first man had reappeared, looking grim.

'What have they done?' John demanded.

'There has been a burglary,' the policeman said slowly. 'But this certainly wasn't someone seizing an opportunity. This was a very specialised burglary. Would you like to come in?'

They trooped after him into the entrance hall and then halted and gazed round unbelievingly. The big mahogany doors which had led into the Hall's main rooms were gone, taken from their hinges, and the doorways gaped open. In the lounge, dining-room and library, ugly brick scars showed on walls where the ornate Victorian fireplaces had stood. As Emma looked round disbelievingly, she saw that in the hall itself there were marks where attempts had been made to lever the two circular plaques of cherubs from the walls.

'Why should anyone do this?' Emma wailed.

The policeman who had searched the house shook his head. 'There's a worldwide market for fine architectural furnishings. Your fireplaces and doors have probably started on a journey abroad already.'

He looked at John Burroughs. 'This young lady could do with a hot drink. Shall we go to the kitchen?'

At the kitchen table the policeman's notebook appeared. 'This burglary must have been carefully planned for when you were out of the house. Now, can you tell me what you have been doing today?'

Briefly she went through what she had done, giving the times when the house was empty.

'And you got back about ten minutes before you called us?'

'Yes.' Then she remembered the lorry driving fast, away from Park Hall, but reluctantly had to admit that she remembered few details about it and would not be able to identify it.

'A pity. It could well have been the thieves. It does look as though they had to leave quickly for some reason, or they wouldn't have left the plaques.'

When darkness finally fell Emma was exhausted. Scene-of-crime officers had examined the rooms for fingerprints and other signs of the thieves and she had had to confirm exactly what was gone and try to find old photographs which showed the doors and fireplaces. John Burroughs had stayed with her, urging her to go to a hotel for the night or ask a friend if she could stay with them. Finally she turned on him.

'I don't want to go anywhere! This is

my home and it's been damaged because I left it! Now all I want to do is go to sleep in my own bed, so please go away!'

He left with great reluctance, looking at her reproachfully and she was able to sink down and confront the suspicion which had been growing ever since she saw the damage.

One man had arranged for her to be away from Park Hall that day, had tried to delay her return and could have called the thieves to let them know that Emma was returning earlier than expected. That man was a wheeler and dealer who knew in details what was left in Park Hall and what would sell quickly.

He also had the facilities to transport heavy objects from place to place. The man who had made her laugh and forget her troubles, who had warned her against trusting people too easily. Was Jed Riley the man who had organised the burglary?

6

Emma slept badly, often waking with a start to listen for sounds which might indicate the return of the burglars. The police officer had commented disapprovingly on the fact that there was no burglar alarm.

'A big house like this, away from any neighbours, needs an alarm system where the police will be notified as soon as there is a break-in.'

'I know, but my father never got round to it,' she said apologetically.

'Well, at least you could get a dog,' were his last words.

At last Emma gave up the attempt to sleep and sat in the kitchen till dawn broke. She felt absurdly reassured by the light coming through the curtains. After all, the burglars had come in broad daylight. At what she thought was an acceptable hour she telephoned

John to apologise for sending him away so rudely the previous evening.

'I understand,' he reassured her. 'Now, is there anything I can do for you today?'

'You could come round this evening and cheer me up,' she suggested shyly. 'I could cook something for supper.'

'Then I'll bring the wine.'

Later Emma called Mr Stanford, told him about the burglary, and arranged to see him before lunch.

'I shall be grateful if you will look up the necessary details so that I can claim on the insurance,' she told him.

There was a brief pause.

'I'll do that,' Mr Stanford said slowly. 'I just hope it's all in order.'

Emma heard the warning note in his voice and was therefore prepared for his solemn face when he greeted her at his office. 'Bad news?'

'Very bad news, I'm afraid,' he said heavily. 'Your father did not pay any premiums for the past two years. There is no insurance.'

Emma slumped back in her chair. Could anything else go wrong? Now she could not even afford to have new doors fitted. Mr Stanford fiddled with his pen, but had obvious difficulty in finding anything comforting to say, and simply murmured a few disjointed phrases.

'Well, at least I'll have something to tell John tonight,' Emma said with false gaiety, pulling herself together and standing up, conscious that there was no point in prolonging the interview.

'Are you seeing John?' Mr Stanford asked with interest, perking up a little. 'He's a bright young man, my nephew. You could do a lot worse than follow any advice he gives you.'

She remembered what he had said when she greeted John that evening. 'We will have to eat in the kitchen, I'm afraid, but at least it's got a door.'

'Who cares about doors?'

'I do! It's very draughty without them.'

It was a simple meal of lamb chops

followed by strawberries and cream, but Emma had enjoyed preparing what she thought of as 'proper' food, rather than the bland, easily-digestible dishes that her father had required. She also enjoyed the fuss that John made of her, his anxious enquiries about how she felt and whether the police had made any progress yet.

'I haven't heard from them. They obviously thought not having an alarm was asking for trouble, anyway. Perhaps I will get a dog.'

'Is there any point? After all, if you are not staying here . . . '

His voice trailed away as he looked at her cautiously, but she smiled wryly.

'It's all right. I won't attack you. I haven't told you yet that your uncle had to tell me that I can't even claim on the insurance, as my father hadn't paid the premiums. I just can't see any way I can afford to stay here now.'

She sighed, and busied herself making the coffee to conceal her distress. 'Shall we have coffee upstairs?'

The room had once been a dignified and beautiful drawing-room. Now the walls were stained where rainwater had penetrated via a rotting window frame and only a small rug lay isolated on the bare floorboards. However there were two old but comfortable armchairs and a small table to hold the coffee.

Emma settled herself in one chair, gazing out over the gardens. 'This used to be my favourite bit of the day. My father was usually watching television, so I could sit here for half an hour or so and watch the sun set over the trees.'

'But now you can choose what to do with your whole life. You are no longer limited to snatching a few minutes for yourself.'

'You're telling me that it's time I moved on. But my family have lived here for a hundred-and-fifty years, John, and from the moment I realised that fact I assumed that it would always be my home.'

'Didn't you expect to marry and move away?'

'Possibly for a time. But I knew that as the only child I would inherit Park Hall, and somehow I thought that I would come back here.'

'But that is impossible now,' he said with a touch of impatience, and she smiled sadly at him.

'I told you that I am coming to accept that. It doesn't mean I have to like it.'

He put his cup down on the table and leant towards her.

'Perhaps you wouldn't feel so bad if you realised how you might benefit from giving it up.'

He felt in his jacket pocket and drew out some papers. 'Two pieces of news that I've been waiting to tell you. The paperwork has come to me because I said I was representing you. First of all, planning permission has been given to build on the grounds and I informed the developers as soon as I got the letter. I heard from them today. Look!'

He spread some sheets of paper on

the table between them and she started to read.

'It sounds very cautious,' she commented. 'They say they won't commit themselves until they have checked various points and they want to carry out a full structural survey of the house.'

'Don't worry about that! Look at what they are offering to pay!'

He pointed to a paragraph on the second page. Emma read it, read it again, and then looked at John with incredulity.

'That's a lot of money!'

He smiled triumphantly. 'And that's not a firm figure, just their first offer! Wait till I've worked on them a bit. You're going to be a rich woman, Emma!'

She enjoyed the thought for a moment, then shook her head. 'I'll get what is left after all the debts have been paid.'

'I'm sure there will be plenty left.'

John left about ten, instructing her to

be careful to lock all the doors and windows as soon as he had gone.

'There's no point! There's nothing left to steal!'

'Nevertheless, do as I tell you. There may be some would-be burglars who don't know the house has been stripped.'

'Very well, sir. I'll do as you say.' She laughed up at him.

He put his hands on her shoulders and she lifted her face to his. It was not a passionate kiss, and her heart did not start beating more quickly, but it was tender and warm. She moved closer to him, but he released her and smiled.

'Good night, Emma Digby. Sleep well.'

As she tidied and washed up, Emma thought about that last minute together. It had not been her first kiss — there had been early experiments at sixth-form dances and a couple of enjoyable flirtations at college before she was summoned home by her father's illness — but she was aware that John's kiss had signalled that their relationship had moved on a step.

The next day saw her return to Mr Stanford and informed him of the developers' offer.

'You know how much my father owed, Mr Stanford. How much will be left when everything is paid?' she said cheerfully, but her face fell when he finished the calculations and told her.

'Is that all?'

'It's the mortgage on the house that is going to take the largest chunk of it. Fortunately I can now tell the company that you will definitely be paying what is owed before long. They were beginning to point out that they could seize the property and sell it to recover their money. At least you won't have to face that now.'

'Well, that's one good thing,' she sighed, and then shrugged. 'At least I should have enough to be able to support myself while I finish training as a teacher.'

'If that is what you want to do.'

But did she? Emma was considering this as she walked home. She had started to train as a teacher because she had no particular desire to do anything else, but at that time she had thought she was a rich heiress and that a career was just going to be something to occupy her, not an essential means of earning a living.

Now she was wondering whether she actually wanted to spend the next forty years teaching young children. Emma resolved to start looking through job advertisements to see if anything attracted her.

She was at least free to go anywhere in the country, or abroad, for that matter. The money left after her father's debts were paid would only be a fraction of the sum the developer was paying, but it would be enough to enable her to choose where she wanted to go. She could even afford a holiday if she wanted to!

She opened the door later in response to a knock, and found John on the doorstep, smiling and offering her a bouquet of summer flowers. She took them with delight, thanked him warmly, and kissed him on the cheek.

'Do you know, this is the first time a man has brought me flowers?'

'Then I must do it again. Now, how about a drive out and afternoon tea somewhere?'

'A very good idea!'

A garden centre provided a pleasant tea shop as well as a chance to admire exotic plants. John was amused as Emma hesitated between a slice of chocolate cake and a scone.

'Why not have both? You can afford it now!'

She shook her head sadly and his smile vanished as he sat bolt upright.

'Why? What's the matter? You haven't changed your mind about selling, have you?'

'No, I'm afraid Park Hall will definitely have to be sold. But I went to see your uncle again yesterday, and unfortunately the debts will take all but a few thousand.'

John was frowning heavily now. 'I didn't realise your father had lost so much.'

'The more he lost, the more he bet the next time in an effort to get his money back. Towards the end he was betting in thousands, and his gambling debts seem to have been the only debts he paid in the last few months.'

He was still frowning, all his attention apparently focussed on stirring his tea carefully. Emma felt a chill. Had the money he believed she would get been so important to him? But as he looked up and smiled at her that thought was forgotten.

'Then we'll just have to hope you find buried treasure in the garden. I'll try and borrow a metal detector.'

It was a pleasant afternoon, though he refused her invitation to come in when they drove back to Park Hall, pleading pressure of paperwork.

As she closed the door the telephone started to ring. 'Jed Riley here,' a voice said cheerfully. 'As you enjoyed the auction the other day I thought you might like to go to a fine arts sale in Chester tomorrow and see how different that can be. Shall I pick you up about eleven?'

There was a moment when Emma's impulse was to say 'yes'. She had enjoyed Jed's company. But then she looked around at the empty door frames and remembered her suspicions.

'I'm afraid I am busy tomorrow,' she said coldly.

There was a pause. Obviously Jed had expected a warmer reaction. 'Well, there is a preview for another sale.'

'I'm afraid I am busy then.'

'I haven't told you when it is!'

She took a deep breath. 'I am busy whenever you want to take me out.'

There was a longer pause. 'I understand.' Now his voice was as cold as hers had been.

'I liked you,' Jed went on. 'I thought we got on well together, but I suppose John Burroughs is more your type. Goodbye.'

'Wait!' she said urgently. 'I need your address. When I get the cheque from the auction I need to know where to send your commission.'

The only response was the sound of the receiver at the other end being put down with considerable force.

Emma spent some time persuading herself that she had done the right thing, but was gloomily aware that she had very little reason really to suspect Jed Riley.

During the following few days she had to admit that now she had been forced to take the decision to sell Park Hall, a load had been lifted from her mind. Resigned to the loss of her family home, she began to look forward. If she decided to return to teacher training she would have nearly a year to fill, as it was unlikely that the sale would be completed before the autumn.

It might be a good idea to acquire some skills which could be used in other work, so she sent off for brochures on secretarial courses, but was more attracted by the idea of working abroad.

She became aware that her intention to sell her home was becoming common knowledge when Stella Shelley knocked at the door one afternoon, looking very self-righteous.

'I am here as representative of a group of concerned residents,' she informed Emma, who had resignedly asked her in. 'We had a meeting the other night after we heard that you intend to sell Park Hall for building land. We were appalled by the news. Park Hall may belong to you legally, but it is part of our local heritage and we are all concerned with its fate.'

'So what do you want me to do?' Emma enquired sweetly.

'We want you to preserve the estate. Ideally we would like to see it restored. The grounds have been badly neglected.'

'And would these 'concerned residents' help me to do this?'

Stella was taken aback. 'Well, of course you are responsible for your own property, but some of us are interested in garden history and we could advise you on what should be done.'

Emma grew suddenly tired of the conversation. Did the stupid woman really think she would sell her home if she didn't have to? She stood up.

'Mrs Shelley, I appreciate your concern and that of your friends, but the fact is that I am going to sell Park Hall. I have to. There is no alternative, no Plan B, so I am afraid you are wasting your time.'

Stella Shelley left protesting indignantly, leaving Emma in a bad temper which was not improved by an encounter with Mrs Fernley later in the day. They met in the street when Emma went shopping, and Mrs Fernley's thin lips curved in a smile.

'Emma! I've just had to listen to Stella Shelley denouncing you as a mercenary vandal because you are selling up.' She lowered her voice. 'Congratulations on seeing sense. Why should you bother what a lot of fusty historians think? It may make your father turn in his grave, but if you have the chance to make a fortune you shouldn't worry about that. I wouldn't hesitate.'

'Mrs Fernley I love Park Hall! I wouldn't sell it if I didn't have to.'

'Of course. Just keep saying that and perhaps some people will believe you.'

She sauntered off before Emma could think of a reply, leaving the girl simmering with fury. The sooner she could leave this place and never return the better.

7

She poured out her grievances to John when he appeared that evening, and he was comfortingly sympathetic and did his best to soothe her.

'Don't worry about people like that. Soon you will be able to move away and forget all about them.'

'How soon?' she demanded.

'A few weeks,' he said vaguely. 'I'm still trying to get the developers to increase their offer and they are seeing when the building on the site will fit in with their plans.'

As they were walking through the hall, John suddenly looked up and gave an exclamation. 'Emma! There is one thing we haven't thought about.'

He pointed to the two circular plaques on the wall, the plaques that the burglars had abandoned when they were interrupted.

'Those? What about them? They're not worth anything.'

Emma had always been mildly fond of the chubby cherubs which decorated the plaques, even though they were not of great beauty. Over the years they had been painted over so often that the finer details had become blurred, and now grime had collected on every fleshy fold. John, however, was staring at them with excitement.

'The thieves thought they were worth taking.' He spun round towards her.

'Have you got a stepladder?'

Together they fetched one from the garage and he climbed up to inspect the cherubs, scratching at one with his fingernail and peering closely at the edges of the plaques. Finally he came down, dusting his hands on his trousers.

'Emma, these could be valuable works of art. Obviously they need cleaning, but I think that under all that paint the cherubs are marble, not plaster.'

Emma felt excitement begin to rise within her. 'How can we find out?'

'I know an art historian who could look at them and give us his opinion.'

His friend, an earnest young man named Allen Brown, arrived two days later, peered at the plaques, examined them closely, and confirmed that the plaques were indeed marble under all the whitewash.

'It's difficult to say any more,' he said frankly. 'They would have to be cleaned and all the paint removed before it would be possible to judge the quality or date the plaques.'

'Well, I could give them a good scrub,' Emma said doubtfully, and the historian turned a peculiar colour.

'Don't touch them!' he said agitatedly, and then blushed at the sight of her astonishment. 'I'm sorry, it's just that if these are valuable you might damage them irretrievably by treating them harshly.'

'I wasn't going to use paint stripper!' Emma said with some amusement, and saw the young man wince.

'I thought maybe we could get them off the wall,' John interrupted. 'The burglars have already loosened them a bit. Then it would be possible to take them somewhere to be looked at properly.'

Between them the two men managed with infinite care to detach the plaques and wrap them in old blankets. Emma then entrusted them to John, who promised her that he would do his best to find the appropriate experts and let her know their judgement as soon as possible.

That left Emma with nothing to do but wait. Sooner or later she would hear from the developers and the art experts, either directly or through John. Grimly she decided that all she could do to fill in the time was to clean Park Hall. She scrubbed, wiped and polished her way through the dusty attics which had been the bedrooms for all those Victorian maids.

Patches of damp where rainwater had

seeped in reminded her how impossibly expensive it would be for her to put the Hall in good condition. She had wondered if there were any forgotten treasures stored up here, but a few pieces of battered furniture and boxes of cheap books were all she found.

Looking at the novels, once best-sellers, but now completely forgotten, she thought of Jed Riley. If she hadn't cut off all contact with him quite so definitely she could have given these to him for his mother. Emma was surprised to find how much she missed Jed's company after just a few meetings, even though she still suspected him of organising the burglary.

John was better looking, more polished, and altogether more compatible with her, but Jed had definitely been more stimulating. Still, John Burroughs was a very pleasant companion. She realised that other people were beginning to regard them a couple when his uncle rang up to ask where John was one day.

'I'm afraid I don't know. I haven't seen him for a couple of days. Did you expect him to be here?'

'I thought he might be,' Mr Stanford said awkwardly. 'After all, he does see quite a lot of you.'

After that conversation Emma had sat on the stairs for some time, thinking deeply. John had been friendly and helpful, but only now did it occur to her that he had been far more attentive and active on her behalf than a purely business relationship required. Was he, to use an unfashionable expression, courting her?

The kiss they had shared had been pleasant, but there was a lot more to a successful marriage than romance. She would see how the relationship developed.

When the attics had had the grime of years removed, Emma started on the bedrooms — all nine of them. She was beginning to feel very sorry for the maids who had not only cleaned the rooms, but also lit fires and cleared away the ashes as well as bringing up jugs of hot water so that the ladies could wash in the privacy of their bedrooms.

Emma was in the middle of one cleaning session, dust clinging to her sweaty face, when she heard a knock at the front door. She frowned. It was mid-afternoon, an unusual time for John to call. If it was he, she thought, looking at herself in a cloudy dressing-table mirror, he was going to see her at her worst. That would test his liking for her!

But when Emma opened the door she found herself facing a completely unknown man casually dressed in jeans and a sweatshirt. A large white motor-caravan stood on the drive and she could see two faces peering at her through the windscreen. Immediately she was afraid that these were the thieves who had stolen the fireplaces, come back to see what else was worth taking, and her first impulse was to slam the door. She managed to resist this, telling herself that the thieves would never have shown themselves so openly.

'Yes?' she said, scowling at the man on the doorstep.

He scowled back. 'Are you Emma Digby?' he said almost accusingly.

'Yes,' she repeated coldly.

'My name is Simon Jennings, I'm your uncle.' He gestured at the motor caravan. 'Those two are Nicholas and Geoffrey, your cousins. My mother told you about us.'

She stared at him in blank surprise for a few moments while he stood dourly awaiting her response until she blinked and stepped back a back.

'Oh? Are you? I mean, please come in.'

He beckoned to the two youths, then stepped into the hallway and waited for his sons to join him.

'This is Nick, he's fifteen, and this is Geoff, he's seventeen,' he informed Emma. In turn the two brothers nervously shook hands with Emma.

They were both tall and would obviously be well built in a few years time, though now they still had the awkwardness of adolescence.

'Would you like a cup of tea?' Emma offered, wondering wildly what the correct procedure was when yet more unknown relatives appeared without warning. However, they murmured acceptance and followed her down to the kitchen where she put the kettle on and managed to find four mugs.

'Well, this is a surprise!' she said brightly after the ritual of tea-pouring and refusing sugar but accepting biscuits had been gone through.

'The boys and I are on our way to the Lake District,' Simon Jennings informed her. 'My mother said she had been to see you and we thought we should call in and meet you.'

Whatever Mrs Jennings had said it had apparently not made a favourable impression on her son, who continued to regard Emma coldly.

'I'm delighted to see you,' she said. 'If

I'd known you were coming I would have had things ready for you. As it is, I was in the middle of cleaning a bedroom.'

She gestured at her messy jeans and tried to flatten her tangled hair.

'It looks as if it is a difficult place to keep clean,' Simon Jennings said flatly.

She followed his gaze and found he was looking at a brand-new cobweb that had somehow appeared on the ceiling. Her two new-found cousins were also looking at it disapprovingly.

'It is rather a big house for one person,' she said, gritting her teeth. 'Would you like to see round it?'

She began the tour in the attics (at least they were clean!) and worked her way down through the bedrooms, dressing-rooms, the sitting, dining and morning-rooms, the kitchens, pantries and cellars.

'Isn't it big!' Nick exclaimed, obviously impressed, and Geoff nodded his agreement. However Simon Jennings, though he said nothing, seemed to be noting each damp patch and squeaky floorboard. His lips tightened when she explained how the burglars had stolen the fireplaces and doors, but he stayed silent.

Emma took them back to the kitchen after she had shown them the entire house. 'It's too late for you to drive on to the Lake District today,' she told them. 'You must spend the night here. I can make some of the beds up.'

'Thank you for your offer,' her uncle replied. 'We would like to stay here overnight, but it will be less trouble all round if we sleep in the caravan.'

This was a relief, but she still had some duties as a hostess. 'Then let me cook you a meal,' she suggested, desperately trying to think if she had enough to feed three hungry males as well as herself.

'That won't be necessary. Joan, my wife, gave us a casserole for tonight's meal. Perhaps we could bring it in here?'

In fact the casserole fed all four of

them and was followed by a homemade apple pie.

'I'm glad you came!' Emma commented. 'I'm afraid my cooking isn't as good as this.'

'Joan is a good cook,' Simon Jennings acknowledged, 'but she's not very fond of hill-walking. That's one of the reasons we have come without her. The other reason,' he continued, giving Emma a meaningful look, 'is that we don't like to leave my mother on her own for too long. After all, she's getting on a bit.'

'She seemed to be able to cope on her own when she came up here.'

'To tell you the truth, we were a bit annoyed when we found she'd come up here by herself. She should have asked me to come with her.'

Before the discussion could go any farther, they heard a knock at the door, and Emma opened it to find John Burroughs outside.

'John! How nice to see you!'

He blinked at the unexpected warmth

of her greeting. 'I was passing, so I thought I'd call in. Whose is that van outside?'

'My uncle and my cousins. Come and meet them. I'll explain later.'

After she had introduced them to each other there was a silence, as if it was difficult to find a subject in common to talk about. Uncle Simon broke it.

'What do you do?' he said bluntly.

'I'm a financial advisor.'

'Really? And does Emma need a financial advisor?'

John drew himself up. 'I am helping her in certain matters,' he said loftily.

'John has been most useful,' Emma broke in. 'Now, tell us which part of the Lake District you are visiting.'

This brutal change of subject led to a polite discussion on the comparative merits of various lakes, and then John glanced at his watch and stood up.

'I'm afraid I must go. Perhaps I can call tomorrow to discuss things — when you are on your own,' he said with meaning.

Emma saw him to the door, but was unable to have a private word before he left because her cousins came with her, carrying various empty dishes back to their caravan.

That night she lay wondering why exactly Simon Jennings and his sons had broken their journey to see her. Nick and Geoff had been friendly enough, but her uncle, though strictly polite, obviously did not regard her with any great warmth.

She sat up suddenly. Her grandmother would have described the large house and the grounds. Perhaps they thought Emma was rich and had come hoping for some benefit from their relative. Simon Jennings would have realised quickly from the state of the building and grounds that Emma had very little money and perhaps disappointment had led to his coldness. Well, they would be gone in a few hours.

They were huddled together by the caravan when she went to say good morning and did not see her coming.

She caught the last part of a speech by Simon Jennings.

'Even if the place has been neglected, the land is still worth plenty,' he was saying argumentatively. Then Nick saw Emma and the change in his expression warned his father, who swung round to face her.

'I hope you slept well,' she said sweetly. 'Can I do anything to help you?'

'We seem to have run out of milk,' Geoff said hopefully, and she was able to offer them a spare pint.

'We should be ready to go soon,' Simon informed her. 'I'll knock when we are ready to leave.'

Half-an-hour later Simon Jennings was at the door, looking determined. 'We are going soon, but I wanted to have a word with you before we left. I just wanted to make things clear,' her uncle began. 'I know my mother offered to help you. After all, she is a kind and generous woman and she was delighted to see you again. I don't know what you were hoping to get from her, but you have to understand that she has very little money.'

Emma was sitting bolt upright, her eyes sparkling with anger. 'What makes you think I want anything from her?'

Simon Jennings shrugged. 'She came back after meeting you and told us that your father had left you penniless so you were going to have to sell the roof over your head and she hoped you would come and live with her.'

'My grandmother was kind enough to say I could stay with her, but I certainly would not be living on her charity! When the estate is sold I expect to have quite a nice sum left when everything has been paid for. In fact,' she blurted out, 'I thought you might have come here hoping to get something from me.'

Mr Jennings looked deeply insulted. 'And why should you think that?'

'If she told you I had a big house with a lot of land it might have sounded quite impressive. I didn't know she'd told you about my financial problems.'

They looked at each other, and then her uncle's mouth twitched. 'I thought you hoped to get money from my mother, and you thought I hoped to get money from you.' He began to shake with laughter. 'Put the kettle on, Emma, and we'll have a proper talk.'

Nick and Geoff were summoned and told there would be a slight delay so they could go and look round the park, and then Emma and Simon Jennings settled down to a full discussion of her situation. He approved of her resolution to sell.

'Of course you must be fond of the place if it has been in your family for so long,' he said understandingly, 'but at your age you don't want to be tied down to a house than needs a fortune spent on it. It would be a millstone round your neck. Sell it, and if you do come south, then come and live with my mother. She'll enjoy the company.' He looked down, avoiding Emma's gaze. 'I know she has missed your mother. In a way, you could replace Amy.'

The Jennings' caravan finally left in late morning, with all three waving happily to her as it drove off. She gazed after it till it was out of sight. Now she had a grandmother, an uncle and two cousins — a proper family.

8

As Emma expected, John appeared the next day, agog to hear the full story of her new relatives. He listened to her account and then annoyed her a little by warning her to be ultra-cautious.

'You do realise that they may say they don't want anything from you, but that might not be the whole truth?'

'I'm not an idiot. Of course I'll be careful, but anyway I've nothing they could want,' she pointed out. 'Even if they think that I've really got millions hidden away, they are going to be disappointed. I refuse to believe that everybody is trying to get what they can out of me. John, I've found I have relatives I like when I was feeling completely alone in the world. Can't you be glad for me?'

'Well, we'll see,' he said unhappily, and she was so irritated that she nearly snapped back that she would see — he had nothing to do with the Jennings. However, she bit her lip and told herself that she should be pleased that he was so worried on her behalf.

Sensibly, he did not dwell on the subject but went on excitedly to tell her the latest news about the cherub plaques.

'I checked up how much it would cost to have your plaques cleaned professionally, and I'm afraid the cost is prohibitive. You just couldn't afford it. So I've managed to persuade an auction house in Chester to put them in their next fine arts sale,' he told her importantly. 'Of course, we could have sent them to London, but then it might have been months before they were sold, and I know you would like the money as soon as possible. Anyway, there was just time to get them in the catalogue, and they will be auctioned before the end of the month.'

'Did the auctioneers give you an estimate of what they think they'll fetch?'

John shrugged. 'The auctioneer estimated that they were worth five to seven hundred pounds.'

'That would be marvellous!'

He held up a warning hand. 'Listen to me before you think that's a good figure. I think he's being very cautious.' Now he was smiling broadly, his eyes sparkling. 'That may be the right figure for mid-Victorian work, but suppose they are much older?' He paused dramatically. 'My friend said that the Victorians often copied work by Italian Renaissance sculptors. Now suppose your plaques aren't copies, but original Italian work? They could be worth hundreds of thousands!'

Emma was momentarily dazzled by a vision of piles of money, but soon she stirred restlessly.

'But there is no proof that they are anything but Victorian until they are cleaned,' she pointed out. 'And your friend isn't an expert.'

'Allen knows as much as these so-called experts,' John defended his friend. 'And even painted over, those cherubs are obviously superb quality. Now we can't claim that they are Italian Renaissance work, but I've spread the word with a few phone calls, and my friend has made a few contacts as well. All we need are two collectors willing to take a chance and the plaques will make a fortune!'

It seemed like pure wishful thinking to Emma, but John was obviously hurt that she did not share his enthusiasm, so she settled for just listening and nodding at appropriate moments. She found herself hoping that he was a little more hard-headed when it came to giving financial advice to his clients. He must be! Look at his car and his clothes!

'Just think what you could do if they did sell for thousands! It would make up for those doors and fittings being stolen because you could replace them. And if the plaques made a lot of money we could restore the whole house!'

She noticed the *we*. Was John

thinking of himself as an advisor, or did he imagine himself actually living in the house with her? She brooded on this when he had gone, wondering what reply she would give if he did tell her he loved her.

However, she did spare a moment to think wistfully of how marvellous it would be if the plaques did make a fortune. No firm offer had yet been received from the developers, John had told her, and creditors were growing more pressing. The bank had reluctantly agreed to extend her overdraft, but the manager was obviously concerned that she had not yet received a firm offer for the estate and was unlikely to let her increase her borrowing limit.

Anthea Fernley seemed surprisingly well informed about her situation when they met by chance.

'It must be so embarrassing for you,' she said, her smug smile contradicting her sympathetic words. 'You've spent your whole life expecting to be a wealthy heiress, and now you have to watch every penny you spend.' Her cold eyes surveyed Emma's well-worn T-shirt and old jeans. 'I hear you are selling all the fittings that weren't stolen. The house must look a mess. And I remember it being so beautiful!'

'Did you ever manage to get inside it?' Emma enquired coolly, and got a moment of satisfaction from the other woman's angry flush, though later she wondered how Anthea Fernley managed to be so well informed about her affairs.

John often called on Emma now when he had finished work, and the two of them would have a coffee and chat about general matters. Occasionally he would stay to share her light supper, but he always left early in the evening and never made any amorous moves, contenting himself with giving her a rare good-night kiss on her forehead.

Once she deliberately held up her face to his, but he seemed disconcerted and hurriedly backed away. She was not hurt by his rejection and decided that he had no romantic intentions whatsoever, and that that was just as well because she definitely wasn't attracted to him. Perhaps he was just being kind to a lonely young woman. Perhaps this was the kind of attention a financial advisor paid to a valuable customer. After all, at some point presumably he would present a bill for his services.

He arrived unexpectedly one afternoon when she was busy weeding a flower bed.

'Hullo! You're early,' she commented, rubbing the soil off her hands.

'I'm here on a business visit,' he responded, lifting his briefcase from the car, and as she looked at him sharply he nodded significantly.

'That's right. The offer has come from the developers.'

At last! Now she would be able to plan her future! Freedom beckoned! Hurriedly she led the way indoors, but insisted that John wait till she had washed her hands and made a hot drink before he told her anything.

She sipped a little tea and then sat back and smiled at him. 'I'm ready now. Tell me everything.'

He took a large brown envelope from his briefcase and drew out a sheaf of papers which he handed to her.

'The important information is on page six.'

She leafed through the papers, found the relevant passage and read it quickly, then read it again very slowly before looking up at John with bitter disappointment.

'But this is much less than their first figure!'

He patted her hand sympathetically. 'I was afraid you would be disappointed.'

She snatched her hand away and reread the figures yet again, before turning to him to demand an explanation.

'What happened? You told me I should get much more than this.'

He shrugged helplessly. 'I'm sorry,

Emma. I queried it with them as soon as the papers arrived, but apparently the firm has managed to buy a large area of land from a farmer just when it had decided to cut back on house building this year. It might be useful to buy Park Hall for future development, but the developers don't want to spend too much on it, and it would cost quite a bit just to knock the house down.'

'Tell them I won't sell at this figure!'

'If I do that they may decide not to buy it at all.'

'There are other developers!'

He avoided her glare and murmured something about difficulties in the housing market at the moment.

'In other words,' she said bitterly, 'you are telling me I haven't any choice, that I will have to accept this miserable offer.'

'At least it will get you out of debt.'

'Just. I wanted something more, money I could live on till I got a job, possibly enough for a deposit on a small house.'

Now he moved closer to her and put a comforting arm round her shoulders. 'Don't give up hope. Remember the plaques.'

Emma blinked back tears. 'I don't want marble cherubs. I need some real angels to bring me good luck for a change.'

'Believe me, Emma, I'm sure the cherubs will sell for a fortune. Then it won't matter how little the developers have offered.'

Gradually, patiently, he persuaded her that there was nothing she could do to get more money from the building firm.

'I'll get the necessary documents drawn up tomorrow,' he promised. 'You can sign them, I'll send them off, and soon you'll be free to do what you like.'

'So long as I don't want to do anything that costs money,' she muttered rebelliously.

He was still assuring her that everything would turn out for the best when he left soon afterwards and he already had the car door open when an idea struck him and he turned back to her.

'Why don't we go to the auction together? Think what a thrill it will be when the bidders start competing for the cherubs!'

Her eyes brightened. 'I'd love to!'

John smiled smugly, clearly pleased by his success in cheering her up. 'Write it in your diary then. The twenty-fifth of this month. It's only two weeks away.'

When his car had roared away down the drive, Emma went back to the kitchen and soberly made herself a fresh pot of tea. She sat holding her cup and gazing in front of her unseeingly. The sale of Park Hall had been intended to solve all her problems. Any money for the cherubs would have been the icing on the cake, for she could not bring herself to believe that they were of great value.

There would not be enough money left over to pay her way through teacher training. When the house was sold and it was time for her to leave it forever, where could she go and what could she do?

Perhaps she could be like Jed Riley, and live on her wits, making money any way she could, without worrying about the future. He seemed to enjoy his life. But on second thoughts a life which involved criminal activities might not suit her.

The urgent sound of the telephone jerked her out of her gloomy thoughts. 'Emma, my love, it's Anscale here, John Anscale.'

Lord Anscale? Her spirits lifted as she remembered the last time she had met him, when John had taken her out in his car.

'How nice to hear from you!'

'And I hope you like what I have to say! We're having a meeting here in a few weeks' time. All the garden societies are getting together to celebrate a very successful summer, and I'd be delighted if you would come.'

'Do I qualify? My garden is still an utter mess.'

'I'm inviting you as my personal guest because I want to see you,' Lord Anscale said firmly.

'In that case I accept your invitation with pleasure.'

'Good. The meeting is on the twenty-fifth at eight o'clock, so put on your glad rags and come along.' He paused. 'You can bring your young man along if you like,' he said with a notable lack of enthusiasm.

'I'll be there,' she promised cheerfully, wondering why John had obviously made such a poor impression on Lord Anscale.

It was only when she went to make a note of the date on her appointments calendar that she realised that both the auction and the garden societies meeting would be on the same day. She hesitated, but then wrote the details down. If the cherubs sold for a lot of money, she would be celebrating. If they went for a song, the evening would be a consolation, a final appearance as Miss Digby of Park Hall before she left her home for an unknown future.

The reference to *glad rags* was worrying. She hadn't bought any new clothes since she came home to nurse her father, and a quick survey of her wardrobe confirmed her fears that she certainly hadn't anything suitable for a garden party at Anscale Hall. Well she would have to buy something.

That weekend found her trying to choose from a mass of clothes of all colours and styles which were laid out for her inspection. She hesitated, then picked up a simple black dress but decided it was more suited to a winter party so she put it back.

'What are you looking for?' the woman in charge, an attractive blonde with a deep tan, enquired.

'Something pretty,' Emma said wistfully. 'I need it for an evening when we'll probably be wandering out into the garden most of the time.'

The woman surveyed her thoughtfully, then picked up a top and skirt in a riot of sweet-pea colours. 'This is what you want,' she said firmly while Emma looked at the garments doubtfully.

'They look a bit shapeless,' Emma ventured, but the woman shook her head.

'You'll give them the shape. This is a good make. When you put these on you'll be surprised how good you look.'

She held out the clothes and Emma took them, impressed by the softness of the fabric and attracted by the soft colours.

'How much?' she enquired, getting out her purse.

'Eight pounds,' she was told. 'Do you want a bag?'

Emma took her purchases, thanked the blonde, and left the car boot sale. On the way home she tried to imagine Anthea Fernley buying her clothes at a car boot sale, but found it impossible to visualise.

That night she stripped off her jeans

and T-shirt and put on the skirt and top. Then she turned to face the mirror, and her eyes widened in amazement. The fabric followed the contours of her slim body, resting on them rather than clinging. The neckline was a little lower than she would usually have worn, but very becoming. Emma laughed aloud with pleasure.

The figure in the mirror showed a young, pretty and carefree girl. This outfit could certainly be described as *glad rags*! She wondered whether John would like the way she looked, then had a sudden vision of Jed Riley eyeing her up and down approvingly and smiling at her with a flash of white teeth.

The mental picture made her realise how much she missed him. Perhaps she should not have jumped to conclusions so quickly. He had definitely been more fun than John Burroughs.

The day before the auction was to take place John appeared, carrying his briefcase and looking very businesslike.

'The papers have come from the

developers,' he informed her, spreading several closely-typed sheets on the kitchen table. 'If you will just sign here, and here, I'll send them back today.'

Emma took the pen he offered and bent over the documents, then frowned and gave the pen back to him.

'I don't think I'll sign them yet. Suppose you are right about the cherubs and they sell for a fortune? I won't want to sell Park Hall then.'

John looked disconcerted. 'I think you ought to sign now. These big firms don't like to be kept waiting.'

'They can wait a day,' she said firmly, pushing the papers back towards him. 'After all, they made me wait long enough for their miserable offer.'

'Please, Emma,' he coaxed her. 'Let's get it over with.'

'No! Just forget about them and think about tomorrow. The auction will be exciting, no matter how it turns out, and then we will finish the day at Anscale Hall.'

She though the mention of Anscale

would distract him. He had been delighted to learn that Lord Anscale had invited him to accompany Emma, though she had tactfully not told him that it had been as an afterthought. But this time her tactic failed. He still looked worried and there was a thin sheen of sweat on his forehead.

For a moment she weakened. Perhaps she should sign the papers now if he thought it was so important. Then she rebelled. After all, she seemed to have spent her whole life doing what other people wanted her to do. Now, in this one small matter, she was not going to give way.

9

Emma gave up trying to sleep and got up soon after dawn. Whatever happened, within twenty-four hours the future of Park Hall would be decided. The auction would start at ten and the cherub plaques would be sold about eleven o'clock, John had estimated from the lot number.

Emma decided she could not manage more than a cup of coffee for breakfast and then dressed carefully in a neat black suit. She gazed in the mirror, and for a moment imagined herself being interviewed on television after the sale had transformed her into a million-airess.

'One look at this old suit and the viewers will know you need a bit of money,' she scolded herself.

John arrived punctually. He looked pale, with shadows under his eyes, and

Emma guessed that he had not slept well either. He greeted her with a rather forced smile and held the door of the car open as she came down the steps.

'Are you ready for the great event?'

'I hope so,' she replied, settling herself back in the leather upholstery. 'But suppose it is an anti-climax?'

'Not a chance,' he assured her, but she wondered if he was trying to convince himself, and why it should be so important to him.

The auction room was full, with a buzz of conversation as people took a final look at the goods on offer and decided how much they should bid. John's friend, Allen Brown, hurried up to them as soon as they entered the door, his eyes shining with excitement.

'There are some important dealers here,' he muttered. 'Something has attracted them, and I hope it's your cherubs.'

'Can we find out?' John asked.

'Well, we can try and overhear what those two are talking about,' Allen replied, indicating a pair of well-dressed men. Emma's heart gave a leap as she realised they were standing next to her cherub plaques.

'Then let's go over there,' John urged, taking Allen's arm. 'You stay here, Emma, and we'll see what we can find out.'

Deserted by the two men, Emma amused herself by inspecting some elegant figurines, but looked up when she heard her name and found herself looking at Jed Riley. She looked at him with delight, taken aback by the rush of pleasure she felt at seeing him, and for a moment all her suspicions were forgotten.

'Jed! What are you doing here? Are you after something special?'

He was polite but unsmiling. 'This time I'm selling. How about you?'

'I'm selling as well. Do you remember the plaques of cherubs in the hall? I have been told that they might be really special and fetch a lot of money.'

Jed was frowning. 'Those cherubs?

Who told you they were valuable?'

'Well, John thinks they might be.'

His face grew hard. 'John Burroughs? Is he setting up as an art expert now?'

There was an awkward silence. Emma looked at Jed, struck again by his air of vigour, the dark eyes in the tanned face, and realised how much she had missed his stimulating company. Guiltily she thought once again that her belief that he was involved in the robbery at Park Hall had had a very flimsy basis.

'Jed,' she began awkwardly. 'I'm sorry about what happened, about how I behaved. It's difficult to explain . . . '

'Not at all,' he interrupted her, just as she was wondering how she could possibly tell him that she had thought he was a thief. 'It was very clear. You were prepared to be friendly with me while I was useful — clearing things up, valuing things and helping you get some money for them, but once I'd done that I had served my purpose and could be dismissed. I'm not your type of person, not like John Burroughs.'

'It wasn't like that,' she protested, but he turned on his heel and walked away, and before she could think what to do next John and Allen Brown had returned.

'No use. They were just talking about their new cars,' John reported glumly. 'Let's sit down. The auction starts in five minutes.'

They perched uncomfortably on some seats near the back of the room and watched as the auctioneer took up his position, nodded familiarly to various people and then read out the conditions of the sale.

'It will be the plaques' turn in about half an hour,' Allen murmured. 'What reserve did you put on them?'

'Reserve?' John said, startled.

'Reserve — the minimum bid you'll accept.'

'I forgot. I didn't set a reserve!'

Allen gulped, and then shrugged. 'It won't matter. They'll sell well, anyway, I'm sure.'

His face did not show the same certainty, however.

The auctioneer sold various lots at what seemed an amazing speed. Then it was the turn of Emma's plaques. Taken from their setting on the walls of Park Hall, the cherubs looked a little forlorn, but John and Allen leaned forward tensely.

The initial bid was for two hundred pounds, and the bids rose very slowly.

'Why aren't they bidding?' John said impatiently, glaring at the dealers.

Whatever the reason, the bidding reached three hundred and fifty pounds, then faltered, and the plaques were sold for three hundred and seventy pounds. Emma did not see who made the winning bid.

While the two men angrily commented on the behaviour of the auctioneer and the dealers, Emma sat silent and unmoving. Not till the moment the auctioneer's hammer fell had she realised how much she had been hoping subconsciously that John

Burroughs would be proved right, that the dream would come true and the cherubs prove to be the angels who would solve all her problems. But this was the end. Now she would have to sign the developers' contract.

'The dealers must be here for something else,' John commented gloomily. 'Come on, Emma. There's no point in staying here any longer.'

She rose and began to follow him towards the door, then stopped abruptly. Now the auctioneer was indicating a folio volume which his assistant was holding up. Hadn't she seen it somewhere before? Throughout the room there was a rustle as people sat up and peered at the book. Suddenly the air was electric. This was what they had been waiting for.

'The political cartoons of James Gillray, the eighteenth century caricaturist,' announced the auctioneer. 'It's the 1842 edition, in very good condition.' He paused and grinned widely. 'And, as all you gentlemen know, it has been bound together with a number of Gillray's ruder cartoons. Now, what am I to bid?'

This time there was no hesitation. The bids came thick and fast, the auctioneer calmly keeping track of them.

'Five thousand five hundred! Five thousand seven hundred and fifty! Six thousand! Any more?'

The hammer fell at six thousand and five hundred pounds. Emma looked round and saw Jed Riley standing a little distance away. He had been looking for her, but glanced away as she caught his eye. Taking a deep breath, she made her way towards him.

'Congratulations!' she said steadily. 'That was the folio you found at the other auction, wasn't it?'

Jed nodded awkwardly. 'Thank you. I was lucky nobody recognised it then.' He frowned. 'I'm sorry about your cherubs. They were worth more.'

She shrugged. 'What does it matter? I'm going to have to sell Park Hall anyway.'

They seemed to have run out of things to say, and she turned away, then hesitated and turned back.

'I enjoyed that day you took me to the auction,' she told him. 'It was fun, and I haven't had much of that recently.'

He looked startled, and then his white teeth flashed in the grin she remembered. 'Perhaps we could meet again sometime after all.'

'I'd like that,' Emma said warmly, and then hesitated. 'Only I probably won't be staying in this area.'

The grin vanished; he nodded, and then turned away as a dealer came up to speak to him. Emma waited for a couple of seconds, then made her way out of the door and found the car where John was waiting impatiently. Allen Brown had vanished, probably fearing her reproaches for raising her hopes in vain.

'Where have you been?' John demanded, starting the engine as soon as he had taken her seat.

'Speaking to Jed Riley. He bought a book for eight pounds a few weeks ago and he's just sold if for six thousand, five hundred.'

John crashed the gears noisily. 'Why should he have all the luck when you need the money?'

'Because he knew what he was doing,' she thought to herself, 'while you and your friend didn't really have a clue.' Aloud she said, 'What does it matter? Tomorrow I'll sign that contract, but tonight we are going to enjoy ourselves at Anscale Hall.'

By the time he dropped her off at Park Hall his temper had improved. 'I'll be here at seven o'clock,' he promised.

Emma closed the door as he drove off, went into the morning room and sank into a chair. So this was the end. Soon she would pack the few belongings she would need and would leave this house where she had been born and grew up, and she would never return.

Mentally she gave herself a shake.

Park Hall would have been a constant burden, she told herself. Now she was free to shape her own future. She could go and stay with her grandmother for a while. Mrs Jennings would be sure to give her good advice.

Sighing, she went to make herself a sandwich, and then spent the rest of the afternoon wandering through the house, saying goodbye to it. It might be a little while before the developers expected her to leave, but once she signed their contract she would no longer feel that Park Hall was her home.

Later Emma showered, then dressed and made up with great care. She looked in the mirror when she had finished and curtseyed to her reflection. The pretty girl in the sweet-pea outfit smiled at her.

'You look good,' Emma told her reflection. 'I hope John Burroughs appreciates you.'

But John Burroughs had other things on his mind. 'If you sign this contract now, I can take it to the developers tomorrow personally,' he argued, his briefcase on the table.

'No,' she said firmly. 'I won't sign it till we've been to Anscale Hall. Perhaps I'll sign it afterwards,' she conceded, and he had to be satisfied with that.

Because of the discussion over the contract, they arrived rather late at Anscale Hall, and the party was already in full swing. Lord Anscale greeted Emma warmly with a kiss on the cheek, and shook John's hand with noticeably less warmth, then led them into a large marquee housing a bar and elaborate buffet.

'Help yourself,' Lord Anscale urged, his eyes darting everywhere to check on the efficiency of the operation. Another guest claimed his attention and Emma and John each took a glass of wine and wandered out into the garden, where evening seemed to have intensified the scent of the flowerbeds.

Emma had made John promise not to mention the auction or her problems, which left them surprisingly little to talk about. Other people were also drifting through the garden. John's attention seemed to be caught by someone, and Emma saw him frown suddenly. 'What's the matter?'

'Nothing. That is, I thought I saw someone who was supposed to call me, but didn't. Would you mind if I tried to find him?'

He set off in purposeful pursuit, scarcely waiting for Emma's consent, and she was looking after him in some surprise when a voice spoke behind her.

'Have you been abandoned?'

It was Jed Riley, but instead of his usual slightly scruffy clothes he was resplendent in a light suit which looked like the product of a famous men's designer. Emma took a step back and admired him openly.

'This is a transformation! I've never seen you in anything but jeans. I'm rather proud of the effect. And may I say that you look extremely glamorous!'

She swept him a mock curtsey. 'What

are you doing here? I didn't know you belonged to a garden society.'

'I brought the marquee, and Lord Anscale invited me to the party.'

As if his name had conjured him up, Lord Anscale appeared. 'There you are, Jed! There seems to be a shortage of chairs in the marquee.'

'No problem. I kept some in reserve, so I'll get them moved.'

Jed set off briskly, and Emma looked at Lord Anscale enquiringly.

'You sound as if you know Mr Riley.'

'Oh, Jed and I have been in contact a lot.'

'He moves tents for you?'

'He supplied and moved the tents. He also provides the chairs and any other furniture, cutlery, china and glass that are needed as well as a lot of other things. Jed Riley runs a very flourishing business supplying everything needed for events like this except the food, and I shan't be surprised if he doesn't start supplying that as well soon.'

Emma was amazed. So Jed Riley was a prospering business man! In that case he certainly wouldn't have bothered to steal a few doors!

'I thought he just moved tents when people asked him, and bought and sold whatever he could find,' she said weakly, to Lord Anscale's evident amusement, but before he could tell her any more about Jed Riley's business activities they were interrupted.

Anthea Fernley, wine glass clasped firmly in her hand, planted herself in front of Emma. She was dressed in a tight black dress whose neckline was rather too low for the occasion, with a large brooch of red stones pinned to one shoulder. It was obvious from her glassy eyes and her rather slurred speech that she had already had several drinks.

'Well, how does it feel to be homeless?' she challenged Emma.

'What are you talking about?' Lord Anscale enquired sharply.

Mrs Fernley turned to him.

'She hasn't told you? Perhaps she was afraid you'd cancel your invitation if you knew she no longer owned Park Hall. She's had to sell it to pay her father's debts.' She laughed loudly, turning back to Emma. 'And you didn't get a very good price for it, did you? John managed that very well.'

'What do you mean?' Emma demanded.

'The developers did a deal with him. He's going to get fifteen thousand pounds from them for persuading you to accept a price way below the value of the estate.'

'Anthea!' It was John Burroughs, desperately trying to silence Mrs Fernley, but he was too late.

Emma was white with fury as she spoke to the woman. 'What a pity Mr Burroughs didn't manage to find you earlier. Then he would have told you I haven't signed the contract yet!' As the woman gasped and fell back, Emma rounded on John Burroughs. 'And now I never will! I was naïve to trust you, but I won't make the same mistake again. Those developers will never get my land!'

She turned her back on him.

'Lord Anscale, would you please call me a taxi?'

'No need. I'll take you home.' Jed Riley shouldered his way forward and she let him take her arm.

Jed's suit might be designer, but he was still driving his old van, and they rattled along the dark lanes in it for several minutes before he asked her quietly how she felt.

'What do you think? I feel a complete fool!' she said sharply. 'I never had the slightest suspicion that he wasn't being completely honest and above board with me.' She brooded briefly and then said blankly, 'And I don't think anyone suspected that he was having an affair with Anthea Fernley. He is, isn't he?'

'That was definitely the impression I got,' Jed said crisply. 'I should think she is one of the reasons he got involved in a shady deal like that. She looks like a lady with expensive tastes. The rubies in that brooch looked real.'

'But then I'm always being fooled by people,' Emma continued bitterly. 'I thought you were living on your wits, dealing in antiques, shifting stuff around. Now I find you have a very successful business.'

There was a short silence before Jed said apologetically, 'I do move stuff around, though on rather a big scale, and antiques are a sideline as well as my hobby. I was going to tell you what I did, but then you made it clear you didn't want to see me any more. Remember, I first met you when you were at Anscale Hall with Burroughs. I suppose it is a kind of inverted snobbery, but I always play up my working-class image when I'm with people like him.

'And the last thing I want to do if I go to an auction or looking for antiques is to look as if I've got a few bob to spare. The prices would go up, so I do try to look like a Liverpool lad living on his wits and just scraping a living.'

There was another silence before Emma said stiffly, 'Thank you for driving me home. I'm sorry to have dragged you away from the party. Now I suppose you will have to drive all the way back to clear up.'

'My staff will get everything tidied away tonight and we'll move everything off site early tomorrow morning. I don't mind missing the party, because it means that I am taking home the most beautiful girl there.'

Emma stared at him, taken aback, but he continued to look tranquilly ahead. She tried to think of some comment, but ended up sitting silently by his side as he steered the little van towards Park Hall.

10

Jed Riley braked suddenly. 'Now what's going on?' he demanded, staring at the motor home standing in the drive of Park Hall.

'It's my uncle!' Emma exclaimed. 'I wasn't expecting him. My cousins are there as well,' she added, as three figures climbed out of the motor home.

'What uncle? What cousins?'

But Emma had scrambled out of the van and was running to greet her relatives. Simon Jennings greeted her with a kiss on the cheek and then looked over her shoulder at the van questioningly.

'It's a friend, Jed Riley,' she reassured him.

Emma introduced her relatives and as the two men shook hands she saw her uncle raise an eyebrow as he registered the discrepancy between the battered old van and Jed's smart appearance.

'We've been touring around a bit and thought we would call in to see how you were getting on,' Simon Jennings told her, and then grinned sheepishly. 'Well, in fact your grandmother ordered me to come and see you if we were within a hundred miles.' He gazed admiringly at her dress. 'You're looking very pretty. Have you been somewhere special?'

'Yes, but then something happened so I left early. Oh, let's all go inside and I'll explain.'

Coffee was soon provided for all, including Jed, who seemed to take it as a matter of course that he was included in the invitation.

Quickly Emma explained what had happened, and Simon Jennings' capable hands gripped his mug tightly.

'Was this John Burroughs the man we met here? I thought he was a dead loss then. Patronising us just because we had different accents.'

Just then Nick stared out of the window. 'There's another car coming up the drive. It's a sports car.'

'John Burroughs!' Jed Riley said with active loathing, making for the door.

Everyone followed, and by the time John had parked his car and got out he found himself confronting the disapproving stares of the Jennings, Emma and Jed.

Ignoring the rest, he addressed Emma. 'That woman had got it all wrong!' he told her. 'I was going to get some money from the developers, but that was just a fee, and I wasn't going to charge you anything. You've got to believe me!'

'You are lying. Get out.'

Jed and Simon Jennings took a menacing step forward, but John Burroughs stood his ground and there was a note of desperation in his voice.

'You must listen to me, let me explain. That deal is the best you'll get. It's not too late to sign the papers.'

'It is too late. I don't trust you. Go away.'

His voice rose. 'I'm staying here till you listen to me.'

'It's time you listened,' said Jed. 'You've been told to leave twice now. Go back to your girlfriend.'

As if on cue, a black limousine swung into the drive, and as it came to a halt Anthea Fernley almost tumbled out of it. As a man and woman emerged behind her, she stood pointing accusingly at John Burroughs.

'That's the man!' she screamed. 'He gave the brooch to me. I didn't know where it came from.'

As John Burroughs looked wildly from the couple advancing purposefully towards him from the car to Emma and the group with her, yet another car turned into the drive, and this time it was a police car.

John Burroughs' nerve snapped. Suddenly he ran off the drive into the sheltering darkness of the gardens, but Nick and Geoff were quick off the mark, and there was a shout of triumph as they caught him up and bore him to the ground. Two policemen ran towards the sound.

Emma abruptly sank down on the front steps. She felt faint and giddy. 'It's like a farce,' she murmured. 'Who else is coming?' Then she fainted.

She came to in the kitchen with Jed and Stephen Jennings peering anxiously down at her.

'Drink this,' Stephen commanded, handing her a mug. Jed was frowning.

'When did you last eat?' he asked her, and she tried to remember.

'Yesterday — I had some supper.'

'You stupid girl!' was the response. Minutes later he stood over her and insisted she finish the soup and bread he had somehow found.

'What has happened?' she questioned when she had obeyed him. 'Where is John Burroughs, and why were the police here?'

'The police took Burroughs away and the other car followed them,' he informed her briefly. 'I'll find out what I can and let you know tomorrow.' He turned to her uncle. 'Will you be staying here? Will you look after her?'

'Of course,' her uncle returned, and looked down at his niece sternly. 'Now, I'll help you upstairs and you can go straight to bed.'

'How can I sleep after all this?' she exclaimed, but once upstairs she found it took a great effort to undress and wash. Within fifteen minutes she was fast asleep.

It was ten o'clock when she woke the next morning and went downstairs to find Nick tidying the kitchen. He had obviously been given his instructions, and tea and toast appeared very quickly.

'Geoff and Dad have gone into the village to do some shopping,' he informed her. 'Your friend Mr Riley telephoned to say that everything was very complicated but he would be calling later. And someone who said he was Lord Anscale has called twice and said he would call again.'

In fact Lord Anscale telephoned ten minutes later. 'How are you, my dear?' he enquired anxiously, and she assured him that she was rested and feeling fine.

'I'm sorry you had to be present at that scene,' she apologised. 'I hope it didn't spoil the party.'

There was a deep chuckle. 'Emma, my dear, the scene involving you was nothing to the scene a little later when someone recognised the ruby brooch that unpleasant woman was wearing and said it had been stolen from her house a few weeks ago!'

Emma nearly dropped the telephone. 'Then what happened?'

'Mrs Fernley said it had been a gift from your Mr Burroughs, and then the woman who claimed the brooch, together with her husband and the Fearnley woman, set off in their car in pursuit of Burroughs, who had left minutes earlier. I telephoned the police, because it looked as though things were turning ugly. I don't know what happened after that, but I thought Burroughs looked shifty from the moment I met him.'

Emma giggled. 'John Burroughs followed me here, then Mrs Fearnley and the couple appeared, and finally the police arrived. I'm hoping to hear the full story later.'

'As soon as you do, let me know.' He hesitated. 'I gather you are having problems anyway. Don't hesitate to get in touch if I can help in any way.'

She thanked him warmly, and then began the wait for Jed Riley to arrive and explain everything. Geoff and Stephen Jennings returned from the village, they all had a simple lunch, but still Jed did not appear.

'We can't go till we have heard the whole story,' Stephen Jennings told her. 'Do you mind if we wait with you?'

'Certainly not. I'm glad of your company. I'd go mad waiting on my own.'

It was mid-afternoon when Jed finally arrived, driving the old van and dressed in his usual jeans and a sweatshirt.

'I'm sorry I couldn't get here before,' he apologised. 'I had to go to Anscale Hall first, and then it was some time before I managed to find someone who could tell me what was happening.'

Emma and the Jennings looked at him expectantly. 'Well, this is what I've found out so far. John Burroughs thought he was entitled to all the things that go with a very successful career, such as a flashy car and a big flat. The only trouble was, he was thoroughly incompetent as a financial advisor and got into a lot of debt. He tried to gamble himself out of trouble and ended up even deeper in debt.

'One of the men he owed money to realised that the people who contacted John Burroughs were usually quite wealthy, so he persuaded Burroughs to check what valuables they had in their houses when he visited them, under the excuse of telling them what they should do with the things, and also to find out details of burglar alarms, etcetera.

'With this information, the man organised several profitable burglaries. Burroughs was given a few items to dispose of, and that caused the trouble. He had started an affair with Anthea Fearnley, who expected expensive presents, and he gave her the ruby brooch.

'He told her not to wear it because he was evading tax, or something like that, but she couldn't resist wearing it to Anscale Hall, and the owner saw it and recognised it.'

'He helped with several burglaries?' Emma asked.

Jed Riley nodded. 'Yes, and I'm afraid the gang he helped burgled this house. Antique fixtures and fittings can be smuggled abroad fairly easily and fetch a good price.'

'So what has happened to him now?'

'He's been arrested and is 'helping police with their enquiries'. In fact he is trying to save his own skin by providing very useful information about his associates. The police have let Mrs Fearnley go. There is no evidence that she was directly involved with the gang.'

He filled in the picture with a few more details and then rose to go. 'I've got to get some marquees on their way to a couple of weddings,' he explained.

Stephen Jennings insisted on accompanying him to the van and Emma saw them standing talking together for a while. Her uncle came back looking satisfied.

'I like that man,' he announced, before telling Emma that he and his sons would have to leave within the hour.

'We've got to be home before ten tonight.'

Emma said farewell to her cousins with some regret. It was surprising how rapidly she had come to feel at ease with them.

'Remember, we expect you to come and stay with us when this place is sold,' were Stephen Jennings's parting words. She waved them goodbye and then went back into the house, which felt very empty, and looked at the gaping doors and the patches where the cherub plaques had been. She would have to sell Park Hall quickly. Perhaps Jed Riley would know someone who might be interested.

Emma was a little surprised when Jed appeared without warning the following day. She had filled a wheelbarrow with weeds and without asking he wheeled it to the compost heap and then demanded a cup of coffee as payment. They sat together on a bench in the sunlight and talked about John Burroughs.

'I can't quite sort out why he behaved as he did,' Emma said slowly. 'He helped to burgle my house, but he went to a lot of trouble over the cherub plaques, and really seemed to hope I would get a lot of money for them.'

'John Burroughs is a weak man,' Jed responded. 'Apparently Anthea Fearnley met him in a visit to London and got her claws into him. Then when he couldn't bluff his way out of trouble any longer down there he moved up here and met you. I'm not sure, Emma, if he loved you or what you represented — status, the landowning gentry, a family home with a historical background — but I think he was torn between the two of you and genuinely wanted to help you.'

'But he helped a gang burgle my house!'

'He didn't have much choice. They threatened him with a very unpleasant fate if he didn't co-operate with them.' Jed looked at Emma. 'Did you care for him?'

She shook her head. 'I was flattered that an attractive man was paying me so much attention, and I was grateful for what I thought he was doing for me, but that was all.'

She sensed Jed relax. 'Changing the subject,' he said casually, 'I would like to talk to you about the future of Park Hall.'

'I was wondering whether you knew anyone who might want to buy a rundown estate and house.'

'I do. Me.' He held up a hand as she turned to him in amazement. 'Let me explain. So far I have supplied the marquees and furniture and fittings for special events, but I also want to start catering for the events as well. At Park Hall the food preparation and cooking could be done in the kitchen, if some of the larders and cellars were made part of it. A couple of bedrooms could serve as offices. And think what a beautiful place it would be to hold weddings!

'With the house and gardens restored, couples would be queuing up to get married here! Incidentally, I was the bidder who bought your cherub plaques. They can come home.'

Emma's eyes widened. 'I know you are a success, but can you afford to buy and restore Park Hall?'

'I might have to sell off an acre, but my bank would give me a loan for the rest. They think well of me.'

'So do Lord Anscale and my uncle,' she commented.

'What about you, Emma?'

'Me? I think it's an excellent plan.'

'I meant, do you think well of me?'

He was gazing at her intently and she felt her cheeks burning.

'Of course I do, but does it matter? I'll soon be gone from here.'

'I hope not. Park Hall is a big house. There will still be room for us to live here.'

'Us?' Flustered, she started to rise, but he caught her hand and she sat down again.

'Emma, when I saw you at Anscale Hall that first time, I felt as if I'd been waiting to meet you all my life. You've no idea how unhappy I was when I thought you might care for John Burroughs. I hope you believe in love at first sight, because that's what it was for me.'

Emma remembered the joy she had felt when she had seen him two days ago at the auction.

'I'm not sure about love at first sight,' she said with a slight tremor, 'but perhaps at third or fourth sight . . . '

'Perhaps?'

'Give me time, Jed. I'm not sure.'

'But I am!' His voice was joyous, confident.

She tried to laugh. 'Don't be too hasty. Your mother might not like me.'

He grinned. 'She does. Do you remember the day of the fete and the elderly lady who you found in the house? She was very favourably impressed.'

'Was that your mother? Why was she here?'

'I asked her to come and have a look at the girl I'd fallen in love with. She was delighted, and thinks we ought to get married before Christmas. I told her you might fancy someone else, but she couldn't believe that you could resist me.'

Emma's chin went up indignantly, but then she saw that he was laughing at her and she smiled. Life with Jed Riley would be fun.

'Of course this place won't be ready for weddings for some time,' he said reflectively. 'We'll get married at Anscale Hall.'

'Jed! I said I'm not sure yet. I need time to decide.'

He seized both her hands. 'How much time? A week? Two weeks?'

She gazed at him with mock dignity. 'I want to be courted. I want presents, flowers, flattery.'

He looked thoughtful.

'Would you settle for an antique clock? There's one coming up at an auction next week, and I think I can get it cheap.'

She pulled her hands away and aimed a blow at him, but he laughed and took her in his arms.

'I'll try and give you whatever you want. I can give you your home for a start, but at least you can be sure that you have my love, now and for always.'

And then he kissed her.

We do hope that you have enjoyed reading this large print book.

Did you know that all of our titles are available for purchase?

We publish a wide range of high quality large print books including:
Romances, Mysteries, Classics
General Fiction
Non Fiction and Westerns

Special interest titles available in large print are:
The Little Oxford Dictionary
Music Book, Song Book
Hymn Book, Service Book

Also available from us courtesy of Oxford University Press:
Young Readers' Dictionary
(large print edition)
Young Readers' Thesaurus
(large print edition)

For further information or a free brochure, please contact us at:
Ulverscroft Large Print Books Ltd.,
The Green, Bradgate Road, Anstey,
Leicester, LE7 7FU, England.
Tel: (00 44) **0116 236 4325**
Fax: (00 44) **0116 234 0205**

HER HEART'S DESIRE

Dorothy Taylor

When Beth Garland's great aunt Emily dies, she leaves Greg, her boyfriend, in Manchester — along with her successful advertising job — to return to live in Emily's cottage. Feeling disillusioned with Greg and his high-handed attitude, she finds herself more and more attracted to her aunt's gardener, Noah. But Noah seems to be hiding from the past, whilst Greg has his own ideas about the direction of their relationship. Surrounded by secrecy and deceit, how will Beth ever find true love?

PRECIOUS MOMENTS

June Gadsby

The heartbreak was all behind her, but hearing her name mentioned on the radio, and that song — their special song — brought bittersweet memories rushing back through the years. It had to be a coincidence, and was best forgotten — but then Lara opened the door to find her past standing there. The moment of truth she had dreaded for years had finally arrived, and she wasn't sure how to handle it . . .